W9-BWB-126

WITHDRAWN

K. J. Parker

This special signed edition
is limited to 1000 numbered copies.

This is copy 908.

MY BEAUTIFUL LIFE

MY BEAUTIFUL LIFE

K. J. PARKER

Subterranean Press 2019

First Edition

ISBN
978-1-59606-930-5

Subterranean Press
PO Box 190106
Burton, MI 48519

subterraneanpress.com

Manufactured in the United States of America

THIS STORY IS based, with a few gross exaggerations, on real events that took place long ago (in the 11th century CE) in an empire far, far away. I wouldn't swear to the accuracy of the entire text in a court of law, but it's definitely as true as most of the stuff you read in the newspapers.

I'VE done some truly appalling things in my life. I'm bitterly ashamed of them now. Saying I did them all for the best—and saying, those things weren't my idea, other people made me do them, is just as bad, admitting that I'm a spineless coward as well as morally bankrupt. I'm a mess, and no good nohow.

I can say all that and get away with it; you can't. Don't even think about it. If you were to repeat what I've just told you word for word, let alone paraphrase it or add a few rhetorical flourishes of your own, they'd have you up for high treason and stretch your neck. Speaking ill of me is slandering the Crown, therefore by implication the Empire, therefore by implication the eight million people who live in it. Quite probably, Bemba—that's the poor devil I'm dictating this to—is guilty of a capital crime just because he's writing down what I told him to—though of course, if he'd refused, that would've been treason too.

It's treason because the Law assumes that anything nasty or bad about the Emperor can't possibly be true; which says an awful lot about the Law and laws in general, if you ask me. I'd write it all out myself and avoid the risk of yet another innocent man going to the gallows for my sake, only I never learned to write, and it's far too late now.

ONCE UPON A time—

Bemba's shaking his head at me; you can't start a history, even an unofficial one, with *once upon a time*. Screw him—sorry, Bemba, I didn't mean that. But *once upon a time* it's going to have to be, because that's the only way I know to start a story, never having had any education to speak of. You can fiddle with it later if you like.

Once upon a time, there were three brothers.

WHERE WAS I?

I've really had enough of the pain. It's always there. You think you've got used to it, up to a point, and then it suddenly flares up and reduces you to a snivelling heap. For crying out loud, says the little voice inside me, pull yourself together, try and preserve the little dignity you've got left, there are people watching you. And besides, adds the little voice, perfectly correctly, you brought all this on yourself, it's all your own fault, like everything else. And whatever you do, don't you dare ask for sympathy.

Fine. But it's a real pest, because it snaps my train of thought like a carrot and I can't concentrate worth a damn, and when I get one of the bad attacks it wipes my mind clean, so I can barely remember who I am. No bad thing, in a way.

All right, let's start again. This is the story of my life, which is shortly going to end, and about time too. I guess you could call it a confession. There's a difference of opinion among the leading theologians on this point. Some of them say you can confess your sins silently, without actually moving your lips, while others maintain that in order to be valid, a confession must be made out loud, *to* someone, or it doesn't count. A third school maintains that that someone has to be a priest, but I have my doubts about that, mostly because priests get paid for hearing confessions. My brother Nico, when he was High Precentor, charged four hundred thousand solidi just for *bless me, father, for I have sinned,* and if you wanted to give him chapter and verse it was extra, fifty thousand solidi per hundred words. I remember saying to him, Nico, you can't charge that much, nobody's going to pay that when a friar'll give you absolution for a solidus fifty. He laughed at me. He was right, too. He got so much business that towards the end, he was actually turning people away.

My brother Nico was a bad man, perhaps the most evil human being I've ever met. He loved me more than anyone or anything in the world. I miss him.

Once upon a time there were three brothers.

The Empire functions on the basis that heredity is everything. Eldest sons inherit from eldest sons. All of us inherit the fruits of the wisdom and valour of our ancestors, who by definition were a hundred times better and smarter than we could ever hope to be. We live in enlightened comfort because our forefathers conquered the world and then made sense of it; we in turn are entitled to enjoy our legacy, because we are the end product of five thousand years of thoughtful, selective breeeding, we're the distilled essence of our ancestors, which must mean we're pretty damn near perfect—none of our doing, of course, it's just a fact. We are what we were bred to be.

But the three brothers weren't born inside the Empire, nor were they citizens. Their mother was beautiful, charming and friendly for a living, and if she knew who their fathers were, she neglected to mention it. There's a remote possibility that one of them was a nobleman in disguise, a prince of the Blood Royal, or maybe even the Invincible Sun Himself, in mortal guise, like in the fairy tales. It'd be nice if that was true, because then the fact that one of the three brothers became Emperor wouldn't be a glaring insult to everything we believe in, but I'm inclined to doubt it.

The three brothers lived with their mother in a wattle-and-daub hut in a village in the mountains. They didn't have any land of their own, not even a scrap of garden to grow cabbages in, so life was something of a struggle when they were growing up. By the time the eldest boy was twelve, their mother was still charming and friendly but no longer beautiful enough to be worth money, so she made her sons sit down one evening and talked to them seriously. Because we're so poor, she said, one of you three will have to be sold. I love you all very much, so I can't possibly decide, you'll have to sort it out among yourselves.

The middle and younger brothers burst into tears, but the eldest brother didn't hesitate. Don't worry, he said, I'll go. I'm the oldest, it's my duty.

The other two agreed. They were very upset, because they loved their brother, and he was big and strong, and protected them from the other kids, and stole things for them to eat when they were hungry. But they didn't want to be sold, so apart from crying a lot they raised no objections.

If you wanted to be sold, you had to go to the fair at Kalenda Maia. Buyers came to the fair from all over, Scheria and the Vesani republic as well as the Empire. A week before it was time to leave for the fair, the eldest brother went out early and didn't come back. The other two were very sad; they figured he'd changed his mind and made a run for it. They didn't blame him—it was exactly what they'd have done if they'd been chosen—but it meant one of them would have to be sold instead, which they didn't fancy at all. They would have tossed a coin for it, but they didn't have a coin. They asked their mother to choose, but she'd recently been paid for her friendliness with a small barrel of brandy and wasn't up to making decisions.

I know, I said. Let's get the Invincible Sun to choose for us.

My brother Edax didn't believe in the Invincible Sun. At least, he didn't deny that He exists—he was a peasant, his mind simply couldn't conceive of something like that, we're alone in the universe and there's nobody up there at all, just clouds—but he figured that Heaven didn't give a shit about us. He said as much, so I picked up a rock and hit him. It's very important to nip blasphemy in the bud. You bloody fool, he said, look what you've done. It'll heal up, I assured him (and I was right, up to a point, but the scar makes people wince when they see it, even now) and don't you dare talk like that ever again. He looked at me, then grinned. It'll have to be you now, he said. Who's going to pay good money for a kid with only one eye?

He was exaggerating, of course, but the point was a valid one. I couldn't argue, and he started to laugh. I wanted to hit him again, but I was too scared by what I'd already done. So I patched him up as best I could with plantain boiled in water and a needle and thread. He whined like hell. I didn't do a very good job, because he kept wriggling and flinching.

The next evening, the day before the fair, Nico came back. He was white as a sheet and his clothes were brown with dried blood. Where the hell have you been, we asked him.

He explained. He'd been told that eunuchs fetch twice as much as whole kids at Kalenda fair, and he figured, if he was going to be sold, why not get the best possible price? So he went to see the stockman at the next-door farm, who told him he was crazy and chased him away. So, being Nico, he sat down under a tree somewhere quiet and thought about it, figured out what to do, from first principles. Then he sharpened his knife—call it a knife; it was three inches of broken blade he'd found in a hedge when he was six—and lit a small fire, and threw a couple of biggish stones on it to heat up. Then he cut off his dick, as far up the shaft as he could manage.

He said he hadn't imagined there'd be that much blood. It gushed out like water from a split pipe, he told me later, and for a moment he was really scared. The idea was to cauterise the cut with one of the hot stones, but he tried to pick the stone out of the fire using two sticks and it kept slipping out again, and by this time there was blood everywhere and he could feel himself draining away, a bit like being drunk, a bit like feeling very, very sleepy; so he grabbed the stone out of the red embers, but he couldn't hold it, and it fell out of his hand, and then he passed out.

He came round in a sort of swamp, where the blood had soaked away into the leaf-mould, like a pig's wallow. He was so weak he could scarcely breathe. But he looked up and saw the sun was a lot further round that it had been, so time was getting on… And then it occurred to him that maybe he'd been out for a long time, maybe a whole day, maybe more, and for all he knew, he'd missed Kalenda fair, and one of us had had to be sold instead. So he got up and walked back to our village.

When our mother heard what he'd done, she burst out screaming and sobbing and wouldn't snap out of it, so she was no use for anything. Edax and I stuffed Nico full of stale cheese and dried apple, which was all there was in the house, and he said he was feeling much better, which I don't think was strictly true, and then it was time to set off for Kalenda.

I think I said Nico was strong. Years later, I asked a famous doctor and he said that Nico should've died, it was a miracle he survived—and then he paused, because miracle usually means the Invincible Sun intervening to some good purpose, and this was Nico we were talking about. It was extraordinary, the doctor went on, that Nico had survived at all, after losing a ridiculous amount of blood, not to mention the risk of infection, and lockjaw from the rusty knife. And then walking twelve miles up the mountain to Kalenda, it was—and then words failed him. Monstrous, I suggested. And he thought about it for a moment, and nodded. Monstrous, he said, quite.

We got to Kalenda somehow, and the fair was just about to start. You want to get to a buying fair early, before the dealers have spent all their money. We hauled Nico up to the first stall we got to, and they looked at him. Five shillings, they said.

Then Nico explained; he'd been cut, so the price was twelve and six. Let's have a look, then, said the dealer, and Nico pulled up his tunic, and the dealer laughed. Sorry, son, he said, that doesn't count.

To be a proper eunuch, he explained, you had to cut the balls off. That's what gives the eunuch his calm, docile, pleasant disposition, which is what people pay good money for. Simply docking the cock was no good; if anything, it reduced the price, since you couldn't breed from a docked man. Then he asked; who was the clown who did this? And Nico said, I did it myself. The dealer stared at him. Four shillings, he said. Take it or leave it.

We left it. Then we went round all the other dealers, but none of them were interested. He's a big, strong lad, they said, but obviously either very stupid or not quite right in the head; four bob, and that's being generous.

By this point we were feeling very sad. I was practically in tears, because obviously we couldn't go home empty-handed, and three or four of the dealers had looked at me quite hard, and one had offered six bob for me. Edax was sulking at Nico for being stupid, and Nico had started bleeding again, though it was just a trickle running down his leg, like a little boy taken short. Mother's going to be so mad at us, Edax kept saying. And I knew I ought to say, it's all right, I'll go instead, but I couldn't, I was too scared and too selfish, so I started snivelling, and Nico had to tell both of us to shut up.

Then, the very last stall we came to, there was an old man with a bald head and another, very short, with a huge mane of flowing white hair, very fine, like a girl's. By this point Nico was so tired he could barely speak, so I had to do the talking. I explained, and the bald man said the usual, let's have a look, then; and I tugged up Nico's hem. The bald man and the man with the silky hair looked at the mess, frowning slightly. How much do you want for him, they asked.

Twelve and six, I said. The two old men looked at each other, and the bald man whispered something in the other man's ear. Then he looked at me and said, the most we can give you is fourteen shillings.

I nearly said, No, twelve, but Edax poked me in the ribs. All right, I said. And that's how we sold my brother. Simple as that.

THIS QUESTION OF belief.

Nico believed—and Edax too, but who cares what he thinks?—that the Invincible Sun exists, but He can only be bothered with important events and important people, which is why Nico felt justified in charging so much more for an absolution. Sure, he said, you can get one for a buck fifty, but if it comes from some red-nosed village Brother, it won't work, it's useless. But if the High Precentor intercedes for you personally, He will actually hear and take note, and your sins will be forgiven and your soul will be washed clean; and what else could you buy for four hundred thousand that could possibly be worth that much money?

(Bear in mind that Nico never had a day's theological training in his life. He got to be High Precentor because the job comes bundled up with being Count of the Stables. It was useful, Nico told me, because of benefit of clergy. He used to go to Temple regularly when he was precentor, mostly so he could get on with some work during the anthems.)

I disagree. I believe that He watches us all, taking careful note of everything we say and everything we do, and that sooner or later He rewards us and punishes us according to our deserts. That's not a comfortable thought. Actually, it's wrong to say I believe. I *know.* Belief implies there's some doubt or uncertainty about the matter. I know. Trust me.

SOME YEARS LATER, Nico had the silky-haired man hunted down (the bald man was already dead), and before he had him crucified, he asked him; why did you buy me, and why did you pay so much? To which the man replied that he and his partner did a lot of business with the Imperial civil service, who were crying out for eunuchs—there was a shortage, would you believe, on account of peace with the Erbafresc, which meant no more prisoners of war—and wouldn't care particularly about the balls so long as they could fill their quota. And why did you pay more than we asked? Well, the man said, you all looked so sad and bedraggled, we felt sorry for you. Didn't do him any good, of course. At that point, Nico was anxious to get rid of all the witnesses to his earlier life, and the crucifixion—well, he had this mean streak. Always there, under the surface. Just the way he was, or the way the Invincible Sun made him.

Also, Nico found out about the beautiful silky fine hair; apparently, if you have the cut before your voice breaks, you'll never go bald and your hair will be beautiful. The dealer had been done when he was six years old, and never gave it a moment's thought.

But I'm getting ahead of myself. Nico was sold to the Commissioners of the Secretariat, who trained him as a clerk. He took to it wonderfully well. He learned his letters and figuring in no time flat, so diligent, so eager to learn, so eager to please. He always did have a tidy mind, and he always was smart. In no time flat, he was absolutely indispensible in Supply; knew where everything was, remembered everyone's names, knew which forms had to be used for which requisitions, pretty soon he was running the place, while his superiors took long lunches. They were mad as cats when he was poached by the Household, but of course, nobody says no to the Household; and so Nico left the provinces and came to the City. Wasn't long before everyone was saying what a splendid Clerk of the Works he'd make, except you have to be a free man to be Clerk. It's a rotten job, of course, though terribly important and grand, because every crumbling wall, loose roof tile and project overdue or over budget is your fault, which was why they were all happy for Nico to get it. But when Nico was Clerk, there weren't any crumbling walls or loose tiles, and every job was finished on time, under budget.

Now, the whole idea of eunuchs in the Service is, they don't get distracted like normal men do. They don't chase around after women and nobody wants to be their friend, so what else is there but work? But Nico was the extreme, prodigious, monstrous; he started work well before Prime and didn't stop till after Compline, he slept on a bench in his office and ate his bread and cheese at his desk, washed down with water in a pottery cup. Usually the Clerk is loathed and hated by everyone who comes into contact with him, by the very nature of his job—if he wants to get something done, he's got to yell at the man who's supposed to be doing it, and if he doesn't he gets yelled at by the man who's waiting to get on with the rest of the project. But somehow Nico managed to keep everybody sweet and happy, weaving the men and their schedules and difficulties together like withies into a basket—he always could bend people, either by sweetness or force, but at this time he was all honey and smiles, a little bit extra squeezed out of the budget for a bonus here, a job for an unemployable idiot nephew there—like the jugglers who balance spinning plates on top of sticks on the tips of their noses, all done with little imperceptible wriggles and flexings of muscles, but from a distance all you see is a man standing still and relaxed, with a happy smile on his face, while a beautiful, ordered firmament circles serenely around him.

EDAX AND I didn't know about any of that, of course. All we knew was, those two old men put a collar on our big brother and led him away, and we took fourteen shillings back to our mother, and three weeks later she died.

It wasn't long before we wished our big brother was in Hell. Where we lived—don't get me wrong, we worshipped the Invincible Sun same as everybody else does except the heathens, but let's say we didn't get many theologians and professors of divinity in those parts; most of what we believed in we'd made up ourselves, or vaguely remembered some missionary telling our great-great-grandfathers. And one of the things we vaguely remembered was the Book of Abominations; all those long lists of things you mustn't eat and mustn't touch. You'll remember, of course, that men with missing or deformed sexual organs are right up there with shellfish and yellow-spotted mushrooms—but of course, nobody takes any of that stuff seriously any more, not since the Erbafresc came up with langoustines in mushroom and white wine sauce. But we did. Just the sort of thing we loved to hear; because it was a reason, an explanation. Every time the crops failed or the plague came round or the free companies stole our sheep or the Imperial army marched off a whole village in wooden collars, we knew exactly what had gone wrong, some selfish bastard had been eating raw fish or buggering chickens, and we were all being punished for it. It made sense, which it simply wouldn't do without the abominations and the tribulation and the wrath of God. So, when word got around about what Nico had done (himself, with a rusty knife, for *money*) and then our mother had died, call that a coincidence because I don't—let's just say Edax and I weren't popular. Everyone knows that an abominator's family are just as filthy as he is himself. Properly speaking they should have boarded us up in our house and set fire to it, except my mother had cousins down in the valley, and they'd have been morally obliged to make a row about it, even though they'd disowned her.

Letting us live was one thing. Giving either of us a job was something quite other. We had the house; we didn't own it, of course, but nobody else would have dreamed of living there, so the owner left us alone. That was all. There wasn't enough ground out back to grow a row of carrots. Neither of us had a trade, and if we'd been the finest blacksmiths or wheelwrights in the country, nobody would have wanted anything we made. We were useless. I had—well, my advantage, even then, but Edax was a scrawny, evil-looking little runt, looking just the way you'd expect an abomination to look. We had no money, and even if we'd had plenty, nobody would've sold us a sack of mouldy oats. We were a problem that would solve itself, given time, and not much time, at that.

(My advantage. I was a tall, thin, skinny kid, but around the time we lost Nico, I started filling out. People say that—for a while—I was the best-looking man in the Empire. I don't believe that, not for one moment. But I was handsome, or pretty, or somewhere between the two. Not that I knew it. We didn't have mirrors where I come from, and how often do you stop and gaze into a bucket of water?)

I remember Edax looking at me, the day we realised there was nothing left to eat in the house, and I looked at him back; and then he said, Fine, if we're evil and damned already, why not? Not usually given to saying clever or perceptive things, my kid brother, but—well, it made me feel a whole lot better about the idea. So we waited till it was dark, and walked out over the back paddock, through the orchard, out onto the lane, up the hill, through the hunting gate, short cut across the four-acres to our nearest neighbour's barn. Nothing was locked or barred, needless to say, so we simply helped ourselves.

Then we went home, stopping to rest a few times along the way because of the weight of what we were carrying, and gorged ourselves silly on barley porridge, roots and store apples. And we waited. I think we both expected the neighbours to come crashing in through the door with dungforks and a noose; but morning came, and then afternoon and evening. They can't have noticed yet, we said to each other, how often do people check their barns to see if the stuff's still all there? Days passed, nobody came by. We finished up the last of what we'd stolen, so we went back for some more.

To find new two-inch-board shutters on the windows and a new door, all fastened with padlocks, the Mezentine pattern with a key that looks like a comb. So they knew we'd been there. Somehow, I think that was what disturbed me most. We were so unclean, they couldn't bring themselves to lynch us for fear of defilement. We smashed a shutter with a big rock and climbed in over the splintered panels.

A week passed; no retribution. But the next time we went there, it was empty, cleaned out. So we trudged on over the other side of the ridge and robbed the priest's tithe barn.

Front and centre with a nice little snippet of theology, exactly the sort of thing you need to know when considering a career in theft. All mortal things, according to the Book of Abominations, are susceptible to defilement, a condition so unspeakable that you put up with crippling loss rather than lay hands on an unclean thief. But the Invincible Sun can't be defiled, any more than you can spoil the sea by pissing in it. And a priest, even a poxy little village Brother, is His agent and minister, by virtue of the principle of apostolic association, therefore undefilable; and the same goes for his duly appointed agents and ministers, their dungforks, their nooses and everything else appertaining to them, under a general license of devolved absolution. They came for us just before dawn the next day, kicked us awake, smacked us around a bit, snapped collars on our necks and marched us, barefoot and stumbling, down to the village, where we saw two ropes waiting for us on the low branch of the hanging tree.

They'd stuck wads of sheep's wool in our mouths, so all Edax could so was mumble and bleat; I didn't bother. We'd done wrong, we'd been caught, and it wasn't as though I'd enjoyed being alive very much, so what the hell. If they'd taken the wad out of my mouth I'd have felt constrained to tell them Edax was completely innocent, I'd done all the thieving on my own; but they didn't, so I never got the chance to redeem myself by penitent sacrifice, probably just as well. They hauled us under the tree, and a couple of men I knew by sight, old friends of my mother's as it happens, came up holding milking stools, and I had a pretty good idea what they were for.

Edax was sobbing his heart out, and that bothered me. I can't say I ever liked him much, there's not really anything about him that anyone could possibly like, but he's my brother. So I prayed; Father in Heaven, please. Now there are learned men who'll tell you a prayer won't work unless it's said aloud, and I had a face full of wool at the time. I can only assume He has a discretion to make exceptions, because just then the Brother came out of his house. He had a scarf wrapped round his face, so only the tip of his nose was sticking out, and he made a special point of not looking at us; we couldn't be hung today, he told them, because it was the old moon before Ascension.

Dead silence. Then someone piped up and said, No, you're wrong there, old moon's not till tonight; and there was a bit of a discussion, until the Brother pointed out that in orthodox doctrine, old moon starts at noon, not sunset—a certain amount of grumbling about that, but you can't really tell a priest he's wrong about theology, not unless you're a priest yourself. So then one of the parish wardens, trying hard to keep his temper, said, All right, but what are we supposed to do with them in the meantime? I'm not having them at my place, that's for sure. Apparently theology didn't have an answer to that, and nobody was in any hurry to volunteer, and there was a long silence, until the priest sighed and said he had a woodshed out back, but someone would have to put a lock on it.

I've often thought about that. I prayed; and my prayers were answered. But how, exactly? The schedule of festivals and holidays is set out in Scripture, written down about a thousand years ago. The phases of the Moon were, presumably, ordained way back at the moment of

Creation, when He set the stars and heavenly bodies in motion. Is it possible that, ten thousand years ago, when He had all sorts of important concerns and difficult calculations on His mind, He spared a moment to factor in the requirement for noon of the old moon of that particular month of that particular year... I find that hard to believe. But even so, I believe it. I believe that from the very Beginning, He so ordered the cosmos and the gearing of the celestial machine to accommodate Edax and me, at that precise moment the most worthless, least valuable articles of livestock in the whole of His illimitable estates. I have to believe it, since the fact is there and irrefutable. I prayed, and we were spared the noose. It happened. Try all you can, wriggle as much as you like, you can't get round it. It's a fact.

No, you fool, you're saying, it's a coincidence. And I forgive you, because I've preached my fatuous little sermon before giving you the other fact; namely, that just after midnight, when Edax and I were lying on an excruciatingly uncomfortable pile of big logs in the Brother's woodshed, there was an earthquake.

We do get earthquakes in those parts; about once every ninety years, as far as anyone can make out, and there'd been one eighteen months earlier, bad enough to shake the half-ripe pears off the trees, misery for the farmers but a source of great joy to their pigs. This earthquake was different. I remember Edax squealing and suddenly shutting up—a huge round of green oak bounced and hit him a glancing blow on the head as it sailed past me and smashed the woodshed door into splinters. Then the shaking stopped, and we sat there, looking at stars through the open doorway.

But not, you can bet your life, for very long. Edax is scrawny, but back then he was fast, and I have long legs. We went sprawling a few times, either aftershocks or we tripped over things, but we picked ourselves up and kept going, didn't stop until the sun rose; at which point it occurred to both of us without the need for words that we didn't want to be seen, so we dived in under a briar hedge and lay there gasping, until I realised (it hit me like a hammer) exactly what had happened, and Edax started whining about being hungry.

THIS MAY COME as a surprise, but nobody seems to know you're an abomination just by looking at you. We made it to Chastel, fifty miles barefoot, walking all night and hiding up during the day, at which point we sort of gave up; either they were looking for us or they weren't, we'd find out quickly enough, but we couldn't go on like that. Turned out they weren't looking for us. In fact, nobody gave a damn about us. And nobody wanted to give us work, either.

So Edax and I had a discussion. We tried stealing, I told him, and it very nearly got us hung. Yes, he said, because we were careless, also it was in the village, where everybody knows everybody and everything. In a city—I suppose I should have explained to him, about praying and being delivered; sort of an implied condition that you don't do it again. But I couldn't bring myself to tell him about that and have him laugh in my face, so I had no valid argument to oppose him with, and as he pointed out, stealing is a two-man job if you want to get away with it, one of you steals, the other keeps a look out. If I abandoned him and he was forced to work alone and got caught, his blood would be on my hands.

But we weren't caught. Not for a long time.

NICO WASN'T CLERK of the Works for very long. There was one of those power-struggles in the civil service, the sort where you get two incredibly powerful and influential ministers who can't stand the sight of each other. To give you an idea; a man I used to know told me about one time when he was out hunting, bow and stable, and he came across two stags fighting. Normally you can't get within a hundred yards, he told me, but these two idiots were so preoccupied with smashing each other to bits that he was able to walk right up close, twenty yards, and shoot them both with consecutive arrows. I don't know if the hunting story is true, but that's exactly how it happens in the civil service. The two mighty stags were so busy clashing horns and gouging each others' flanks, they didn't notice the real enemy until it was all over, and they were sitting in mail coaches on their way to deputy assistant postmasterships in the Perioeca.

Now the man who won the power struggle was a shrewd judge of character and a marvellous operator in the confined spaces of the Chancery corridors; he wasn't quite so hot on which form to use for which application, and when the quarterly appropriations were due in by. Just as well he'd noticed my brother Nico. Stick with me, he'd whispered in his ear, and I'll see you right; and Nico left the Clerk's office and moved into the offices of the Count of the Stables.

Goes without saying, the Count of the Stables doesn't have anything to do with hay, oats or fresh straw. Once upon a time; but that was many years ago. The story goes that Tryphon IV, realising that the nest of vipers who ran the Treasury were out to get him, set up a parallel underground treasury routed through the royal stables, and put the chief groom in charge of the whole thing because he was the only man in the City he could trust. And the chief groom did such a good job that within two years the budget deficit was just a memory and the soldiers were paid on time and twelve billion in taxes that had sort of trickled away into the pockets of the Treasury bosses found its way back into the Exchequer; whereupon the chief groom had Tryphon quietly stabbed and in due course assumed the purple under the name of Basiliscus II. Nice story; quite possibly true. Anyhow, the Count of the Stables does a great many things, but none of them with a pitchfork.

Nor, if you want to borrow a horse, is the Stables a good place to look for one. It's a huge building out back of the Red Palace, with a hundred and sixteen windows and just the one door. Getting round inside it is a nightmare until you've been there a year; and don't bother asking anyone the way, because they'll lie to you. The theory being; if you need to ask, you must be new, and novelty is a terrible sin in the Stables. If you're new, chances are you're either a spy for the Exchequer or a pushy young cutthroat after somebody's job.

Nico, of course, was both. On his first day, some old clerk took him for a long walk, the long way round so as to confuse him, and showed him his office, then walked away and left him to it. But Nico was ready. He'd been counting under his breath all the way; thirty paces, turn left, twenty-six paces, up the stairs, seventeen paces, turn right, and so on. Not many men would have bothered, but Nico was smart, he knew how much it mattered. So, the first thing he did when he was alone in his new lair was to pull a wax tablet out of his sleeve (there was no paper or pen in the office, needless to say) and wrote it all down before he forgot it. For the first three weeks he had to follow the same roundabout route, but at least he didn't get hopelessly lost; and every night he made additions and corrections to the map he was making of the place, the only one in existence; there'd never been one before and Nico made damned sure there never was one again. By the end of his fifth week, he knew the geography of that building better than the men who'd been there twenty years, and he always reckoned that was the key to his later success. Just knowing where everything and everybody was, and who you'd have to go past on your way to talk to so-and-so, and who'd be able to overhear whose conversations—

For his first year in the Stables, Nico was the perfect henchman. The great man whose coat-tails had carried him there relied on him for everything, and he was never disappointed. Also, though he'd said nothing to anyone, the great man's key enemies in the department started retiring early, transferring to rubbish jobs in the provinces or dying. A marvellous run of good luck, he thought for a while, and then he realised that nobody's that lucky, and he must have a guardian angel he didn't know about; and by the time he'd figured out who the guardian angel was, it was too late. Nico didn't say a word; he didn't have to. All he did was leave a dossier on the great man's desk—copy statements, excerpts from the record, letters, memoranda, no big deal on their own but taken together, proof positive that the great man had been systematically blackmailing and murdering his colleagues until there was nobody left standing.

I didn't do it, he protested. It wasn't me.

No, Nico told him, it was me. But nobody's going to believe you didn't tell me to.

So the great man retired—honourably, they made him permanent secretary to the governor of the Snake Islands, and within a year he was dead from malaria—and Nico became the new Count of the Stables, on his predecessor's vehement recommendation. The first thing he did, so he told me later, was to burn the map. He didn't need it any more, and (like the forty-seven high officers of state who Nico's predecessor had murdered without even knowing it) it was too dangerous to exist.

STEALING FOR A living is like falling off a roof. For a while, you sail along, exhilarated by the slipstream, free as a bird and twice as fast through the air, and then you hit something and it's suddenly no good at all.

There was this goldsmith in Roches. We'd taken it in turns to watch his shop from the street, and as far as we could tell there was nothing to worry about; no dog, the old man lived there on his own, no family, no living relatives apart from a cousin two hundred miles away. The door was four plies of oak laid cross-grain, but there was a side window with a shutter fastened with an old-fashioned fist-and-elbow padlock, and Edax reckoned he could deal with that, no problem. He was right, too, for once. He picked it in about two minutes, his hobnailed boots on my poor shoulders, and then we were inside. And we were quite right, there wasn't a dog—we'd have known if there was, because we'd have heard it bark, and seen someone taking it for walks. We were right about everything, as it turned out, apart from one thing.

And here's a bit of very good advice. If you've got something valuable and you don't want it stolen, don't bother with a dog; get a goose. It costs practically nothing to feed, you can keep it shut up in a cage all day, and doesn't it ever make a racket if something disturbs it in the middle of the night. A goose, for crying out loud.

First thing we knew about it was this horrible noise, and something dimly white in the moonlit room, thrashing about. First a sort of blaring noise, like someone blowing through a cow's horn, and then hissing, like a bad play in the theatre, and the thump of the bloody thing's wings against the bars of the cage. Fact is, we were so scared we didn't stop to think; what's that, oh, it's only a goose. We scrambled for the window. I got there first but Edax elbowed me out of the way, hauled himself through, jumped and broke his ankle. A moment later I landed on top of him, and he howled so loud it set all the dogs in the street barking. I scrambled up; he just lay there. Come *on*, I yelled; I can't move, he said. I grabbed his arm, and he howled even louder. It hurts, he said. So I let go his arm, which I'd contrived to break when I landed on him. Don't leave me, he said. So I got my arms under his shoulders and started to lug him down the street, and then the watch arrived.

The watch commander sympathised, I could see that, but he explained; it wasn't up to him, his hands were tied. Theoretically, he had a budget for medical care for suspects in custody, but the fact was, money was tight, the surgeons in Roches were a bunch of thieves and bandits, and there really wasn't any point spending money fixing up my brother's arm and leg when we were both going to be hung in two days' time, sure as eggs. Think about the next poor devil who occupies this cell, he told me. He'll come in here with a broken leg or busted ribs, and who knows, he could be innocent as a new-born babe, and all the money for fixing up injured criminals had been wasted on a dead man, or as good as. I thanked him, told him I could see his point, and asked nicely for four sticks and some old rag. He grinned, came back with a length of batten he'd fished out of the firewood, and two military-issue scarves. I'm no doctor, but

I'd seen a leg set a couple of times. Edax squealed like a pig while I was hauling him about trying to fit the two ends of the breaks together, and it nearly broke my heart. You clown, he told me with tears in his eyes, you're doing it all wrong. Probably, I told him, but you heard the man, it really doesn't matter. And then he called me a whole bunch of names, all of which I deserved, until I managed to get the splints tied down tight.

They had us up in front of the judge the next morning. I did the talking, what little there was of it; names and where we were from, while Edax clung to my arm and sobbed. And it occurred to me to think that I hadn't really made the best use of my life so far, so maybe it was just as well I'd be relieved of the responsibility. It's like the parable, the one about the rich man who goes away leaving his steward in charge of the vineyard, and when he comes back it's choked with weeds and all the crops have rotten. And then the judge yawned and said, death by hanging, and that was that.

It's hard to pray when you're squashed up in a cell the size of a chicken-coop with someone bawling his eyes out. In prayer, you're looking to forget your earthly body and join in metaphysical union with the Eternal, and it spoils the mood if you can't hear yourself think, and someone keeps prodding you in the ribs with his splinted leg. I did my best. Lord, I said, I have no right to call on You. I had my chance and I wasted it. I'm weak and worthless and I can't see any point in going on, but my brother here must love his life or he wouldn't be making that dreadful noise at the thought of losing it; if You could see your way to getting him out of this, it would be more than either of us could ever possibly deserve, but to You all things are possible, and maybe You can find a use for him some day, who knows?

And then I guess I must have fallen asleep, because I distinctly remember the dream I had. I was sitting on a golden throne, and next to me was Edax; we were both wearing the lorus, divitision and greater dalmatic and the triple crown and pendetilia—I knew that's what they were, though of course I'd never seen them in my life—and I held the sceptre and globe cruciger, and across my knees was a beautiful sword; and someone said to me; this is why. And I remember thinking, what could that possibly mean?

In the morning, they came to get us. But there were three of them; the watch captain, an old man with a leather satchel and a short, small man with hedgehog-bristle hair who obviously scared the other two to death. He didn't say anything. The watch captain said; terribly sorry, this whole thing's been a dreadful mistake, you're free to go, and this is the surgeon, would you please let him have a look and see if there's anything he can do? He was sweating, I remember, great fat drops of sweat rolling down his forehead, down the bridge of his nose. And the surgeon, the old man with the satchel, was furious; what stupid bloody fool set this leg, he said angrily, and I said, actually, that was me; and he went all quiet and gave Edax's ankle a little twist which made him yell; a little click, and then he bound it up nice and tight with proper splints and proper new linen bandages. Then they had two soldiers help Edax out of the cell, up the stairs and out into the daylight, where there was a coach waiting; the mail, no less, fastest thing without wings in the world, with cushioned seats and rugs to put over our knees, and a wicker basket with fresh bread, cheese, dried sausage and a bottle of wine.

And I thought; that's twice I've prayed, and twice it's worked.

We were two days in the coach—the mail doesn't stop, except to change horses—and we hardly said a word to each other, mostly because when we were half an hour out of Roches I told Edax to for God's sake stop whining, and he sulked a lot after that. Gave me a chance to think. Where were we going? No idea. But even if Edax hadn't been all busted up, we couldn't have jumped off the mail and survived, and when we stopped to change horses—at some point I think I must have tried the latch on the coach door, and it was bolted on the outside. And then I thought; well, my prayers have been answered, and this is the form the answer takes. Presumably I'm just too stupid to understand.

Then the coach slowed down, and we were in a big city, much bigger than Chastel or Roches, the way a bull's bigger than a day-old calf. So we slowed down, and I saw Edax try the door-latch. Don't be stupid, I told him, you can't run and I can't carry you, and he looked daggers at me and hugged his broken arm.

And then we went under a low arch into a little yard, and the coach stopped, and someone jumped down and shot the bolts on the doors and opened them, and

I stepped out; and there, standing right in front of me, was Nico, except he was wearing a long black gown like a priest. And he grabbed me and crushed all the breath out of me. You idiot, he said, you complete arsehole.

HE'D BEEN SEARCHING for us, he told us later, for two years, ever since he'd got himself well enough established in the Service to be able to look after us and provide for us; but we would insist on moving about and making ourselves hard to find—we were both officially dead, for one thing, except he'd chosen not to believe that (faith; my brother had faith the way a soldier keeps the sword he brought back from the war, even though his side lost and the country's now occupied by the enemy). So he'd paid the best portrait painter in the City to paint miniatures of us both, on little ivory cards—a hell of a job, because he could only remember us the way we'd been when we were still just kids; he kept making the artist stop and scrape off what he'd done and try again. And then he sent his man Gigax (the little man with the hedgehog hair) all round the country with the miniatures in his pocket, have you seen these men? And eventually he found someone in a bar who said yes, but you'll have to be quick, they're getting hung in the morning.

But all that, Nico said, was over now. We were here, and we were safe, and nothing bad was ever going to happen to any of us ever again. And he told us all about his amazing rise to power, how incredibly successful he'd been; it was all for you, he said, it was all so we could be together again, as a family, and safe. After all, he said, what could possibly be more important than that?

HE HAD THE best doctors in the City in to look at Edax, but they shook their heads and said the damage was already done, there was nothing they could do; he'd be lame for the rest of his life, and his right hand would never close properly. That made Nico very sad, but he told me it wasn't my fault, not really, given the circumstances.

I told him about how I'd prayed, and how my prayers had been answered. But Nico just laughed. Don't be stupid, he said. There is no Invincible Sun, didn't anyone ever tell you that? There's just a big white thing in the sky that makes you go blind if you stare at it, and there's Edax and you and me, and that's it. Nothing and nobody else matters, just us.

But Nico, I said, I prayed—twice—and both times my prayers were answered. You idiot, he said. Think about that just a moment. If He exists and He wanted to save you, then surely the sensible time to do it would've been *before* you were right on the point of being killed, rather than leaving it to the very last minute. Better still, he'd have had you find a five-shilling piece in the street, so you wouldn't have had to go thieving. But no, He waits till the noose is practically round your neck, and then He intervenes. If I had a clerk who arranged things as badly as that, I'd fire him tomorrow. Tell you what, Nico said, if your

Invincible Sun ever needs a job, tell Him not to bother applying to the Service. He'd never make the grade.

NICO HAD ROOMS, a room, in the attic of the Stables, though he more or less lived in his office. For us he bought a house on the Savatina, with an acre of garden, and a dozen servants to look after us. Are you crazy, I asked him. He grinned. He could afford it, he said. He could afford it out of a week's pay, and still have change to buy a warship. Then he said; Look at me, what do you see?

I told him, I didn't understand the question.

What you're looking at, little brother, he said, is the second most powerful man in the Empire. And in case you're wondering, no, not the Emperor, he's number three. There's me and there's Cratylus, the Guardian of the Orphans, and between you and me, I'm planning to do something about that.

You've lost me, I said. Nico, what the hell is going on?

SO HE EXPLAINED.

Let me take you back, he said, to when the old emperor died. Basiliscus V, greatest emperor we've ever had; on the throne for fifty-seven years, found the empire in ruins, left it bigger and richer and stronger than it's ever been. He really was a great man, Nico said (and when Nico says something good about someone, without any excepts or apart froms, you'd better believe it) but there was one thing he didn't do which made everything else a complete waste of time. He never had a son.

Daughters, yes; two of them. But no son. Not for want of trying. Basiliscus never failed in anything because of not trying. Twice a day, morning and evening, whenever he wasn't away at the wars, and according to the palace guards you could hear him trying out in the courtyard; but all the empress ever came out with was two daughters, until at last she'd had enough and withdrew to a convent. By which point Basiliscus was an old man, but he was halfway through getting the marriage annulled so he could remarry when he died himself, of lockjaw, and that was that. Because he assumed he'd live forever, and because he didn't want his daughters to marry until he'd produced a son, the princesses were both old maids by then. The elder, Apollonia, had gone off to the convent when she was nineteen and had been there ever since; which left the other one.

Now even I'd heard of her. The Princess Bia; Bia Carbonopsina, meaning coal-black eyes, the most beautiful woman in the world. Yes, Nico said, that's her. But that was twenty years earlier. Twenty years, and she's still there, still a princess wrapped in swansdown and ermine, only not quite so pretty as she once was. Never mind; the obvious answer was, princess Bia had to marry and produce an heir, and then we'd be back on track and everything will be fine.

True, we all said, it's cutting it a bit fine. Princess Bia is, as a matter of cold genealogical fact, forty-five years old;

but stranger things have happened, and the alternative is civil war, so let's give it a shot and see what happens. The princess herself was all for it, of course. All her life, all forty-five years of it, she'd been led to believe that one day she'd marry a handsome prince and live happily ever after, and as time went on, her patience was wearing thin. Didn't help, of course, being a princess and blood royal. Other girls, other women, can usually find ways of amusing themselves, so long as they're discreet and nothing disastrous happens, but not her, because of the unthinkable dynastic consequences. So, she lived in what was essentially a prison, and the only men she ever saw were, well, (Nico said) men like me. Most of the time she spent brewing perfumes; she was really good at it, good enough to earn her own living, and bottles of her choicest concoctions were sent as marks of special favour to queens and empresses right across the world. She, however, never left the North Tower, and she wasn't happy about that at all.

So, when they broke the bad news that she was going to have to marry and breed to save the world from drowning in a sea of blood, she was only too happy to comply. As to who the lucky man was going to be, she had very strong opinions on that. Years ago she'd fallen in love with a handsome senator. She hadn't seen him for a while, but no matter. There had been a slight delay, but never mind about that, either. One day my prince will come, and here he finally was.

Vestinus Apsimar had been every woman's dream when he was twenty-seven and Bia was fourteen; he was still solidly handsome at fifty-eight, so long as he stuck his chin out and his stomach in. He'd been married, very happily, for thirty years, but off went his wife to the convent, along with their three daughters, and Apsimar had a haircut and a shave, splashed his face all over with rosewater, and went to the palace to be married to his princess.

What he found when she lifted the veil was a tall, thin woman with big, dark eyes, and I don't suppose he felt like he'd been ill-used or cheated. She wasn't exactly hideous, and he was to be the new emperor, and the one duty expected of him was something he'd been doing all his adult life, with boundless enthusiasm and a fair degree of skill.

Well, said Nico, that was eleven years ago. For the first six years, Apsimar went about his one duty with all the diligence and sense of civic duty that you'd expect from a son of one of the oldest families in the Empire; after that, I guess, he came to the conclusion that there really wasn't any point to it; and besides, he told himself, the empire didn't need another emperor, because it had him, and he was doing a fine job; and as for an heir, there was always his nephew. So back went Princess Bia to her tower and her alembics—didn't go quietly, so they tell me, and she may be thin but she's wiry, but they got her there in the end—and Apsimar set about being the best emperor in history. Apsimar the Great was what he was aiming at, though he'd probably settle for Apsimar the Strong, or Apsimar the Wise would do at a pinch. And there he still is, and there she still is, and everything would be fine, except—

Except what? I asked him. And he looked at me.

APSIMAR, SAID NICO, lowering his voice even though we were alone, is a pinhead. An idiot. Far worse than that, he's a pin-headed idiot who thinks he's great and strong and wise.

Now, that needn't be a problem, Nico went on. Half of our greatest emperors—Florian III, Cleophon, Artax II—have been pinheads, or drunks, or crazy as jaybirds, but it didn't matter because they took no interest in the job and were happy for the Service to deal with everything for them. Not so with Apsimar. He interferes. First thing he did was have Ninus arrested, tonsured and sent to a monastery. Who's Ninus? Before your time, I suppose. They used to call him Ninus the Weasel. He was a loathsome little man who ran the Empire for Basiliscus when he was away at the wars, and he did it very well, very well indeed. But Apsimar got rid of him the moment the lorus landed round his neck, and that's how come I got promoted from Count of the Stables to Chancellor, because Cratylus, who was Chancellor before me, got kicked upstairs to Guardian of the Orphans. And when I tell you Apsimar and Cratylus deserve each other—

Actually, that's not quite fair. Cratylus is smart. But for the last thirty years he's been systematically robbing the Treasury on an industrial scale—you take a ride on the mail from the City to Trabasc, and all the land you'll ride over belongs to him, through one dummy corporation or another—and he knows for a fact that if he ever loses his grip on power, his head will be decorating a pike in the Square. So, whatever Apsimar tells him to do, he does it, no matter how crassly idiotic it might be, because his only chance of staying alive is to be second-in-command to an easily led clown. Now if I was him, I'd look back and ask myself, if that's the outcome, was it all worth it? Still, it wouldn't do if we were all the same.

How bad? Oh boy. Second thing Apsimar did, he cancelled the protection money to the Robur.

Yes, really. That's what I mean. Even Basiliscus, who never lost a battle, made sure the savages got their money, twenty million in gold, first day of spring every year. There's just too many of them, he used to say, and if we were to fight them instead of buying them off, first, we'd lose, second, it'd cost a hundred and fifty million a year to keep an army on the frontier which stands any chance of keeping them in check. So, what does Apsimar do? He cancels the tribute and uses the money to endow a school of philosophy. Apsimar the Wise. Idiot.

And then Nico sighed, and said; That's why it's so important that we're together, where I can look after you. Trust me, everything's about to go to hell, it won't be long before nowhere and nobody's safe, not unless they're really in tight, where they can pull the walls in round them like a blanket and snuggle down till it's all over. It's not just the wars. The Treasury's empty, there's fifty thousand men out of work in the City alone, rents are so high the farmers can't pay the taxes to keep the army in the field, there's honest men selling their kids, honest men who can't sell their kids because nobody can afford to buy them—from here you'd never believe it, but out at the edges it's all coming apart, and everyone still thinks it's like it was when the old emperor was alive; and it looks that way, because we keep up appearances as though our lives depend on it, but it isn't.

And then he grinned at me and grabbed me by the shoulders. But we'll be all right, he said, you and Edax and me. I've got it covered. I know what I'm doing.

I DON'T LIKE talking about myself, for obvious reasons. I've felt that way all my life. It's always seemed so unreasonable, if you see what I'm trying to say, like a bad joke or a prank.

Doesn't he take after his mother, they used to say when I was a little kid. Then, later; when he grows up he'll be a real heartbreaker (like that's a good thing). Then, later, who's a pretty boy, then, as the other kids threw stones at me, because they were jealous, and I was my mother's son.

Sometimes I ask myself; did my mother pray, when I was born? Did she say, Lord, make him handsome, the best-looking man in the world? And were her prayers answered, or did I just turn out that way because of chance?

The stupid thing is, Edax and I look quite alike—not Nico; big and dark, with a broad face, though he got our mother's eyes. But Edax and I have got the same nose and chin, the same forehead. But he turned out small and scraggy, and I'm tall. And for some reason, the things that look good on me make him look sly and evil. You can't go by appearances, obviously, though people do.

Nico said, and I agreed with him, that the best thing we could do with Edax was keep him indoors, with lots of nice things to play with, so he wouldn't be tempted to make trouble for anyone. What about me, I asked him, is there anything I can do to help? Funny you should mention that, Nico said.

(LATER, I ASKED him how it had been. What do you mean, he said. Oh, that. Well, I can't say it's bothered me particularly, what you've never had you don't miss, and I'm glad to have done without the distractions. It's like an archery match. You shoot the arrow, but it's got a hundred yards to fly, and the wind's blowing on it all that way. You allow so much when you let fly, but even so, it's much better to shoot on a still day. Me, I've never had so much as a slight breeze between me and where I needed to go.

But what about a family, I said, and kids? And he laughed. I've got you two, he said.)

SO NICO GOT me a job as an equerry. To this day—and I have a hundred of them at my command, day and night; lucky me—I have no very clear idea of what an equerry actually does. What I mostly seemed to do was stand about, something I'm not bad at, though I do say so myself. First I stood about in the anteroom outside the Purple, which is the throne-room. Then I stood about inside the Purple, near the doors, at the back. Then I graduated to about halfway up, where I was occasionally called upon to fetch things, or laugh at someone's joke. I must have done that very well indeed, because before I knew it I was standing about at the far end, from where you can actually see the throne, if you're tall and you stand on tiptoe and peek over people's shoulders. And the man sitting on it.

From where I was standing, he didn't look so bad. He was a big man, with a fine head of snow-white hair, a firm chin, piercing blue eyes, broad shoulders, and he sat there with dignity, talking in a low, pleasant voice; and what he said seemed to make sense, except I didn't know the context. Anyway, he seemed to be doing a fine job; just like me, I guess. And he seemed to spend most of his time listening, which always makes a man seem wise; philosophers and scholars and theologians, I couldn't follow most of what they said but he could, or he looked like he understood every word, and every now and then he'd nod gravely. Apsimar the Wise, which would do, at a pinch.

One day, when I got off work, some clerk came up to me and told me my brother wanted to see me in his office. So off we went, up a mountain of stairs and down again, along corridors, down tunnels, up towers, until I had absolutely no idea where I was, though my feet told me I must have walked at least two miles. And then he suddenly stopped, in front of a plain dark oak door looking exactly the same as the thousand-odd plain dark oak doors we'd walked past; no name or number on it, goes without saying. In there, the clerk told me. I knocked and waited, and I heard Nico telling me to come in.

I'd never been in that part of the palace before, and I was under the impression that Nico's room was in the Stables—

That's right, he said, that's exactly where we are. And he explained that there were corridors that ran through the attics and the cellars, all the way from the palace to the Stables—about two miles, he told me—which meant that government clerks could come and go from one department to another without ever seeing the sun, or being seen. I'd have thought you'd have a bigger place than this, I told him, and he looked at me. What for? he said. I couldn't think of an answer to that.

Anyhow, he told me, good news, you've been promoted. Why? I asked him, and I don't think it was the question he was expecting. I haven't done anything clever, I explained, I just stand there. He nodded. Very well too, so I gather, he said, and so they've promoted you. From tomorrow, you're going to be chief equerry to her majesty the empress.

Why? I asked him.

Nico didn't lose his temper, the same way poor men generally don't drop gold coins in the street. She asked for you, he said, by name. But she's never seen me, I said. He scowled. Well, he said, someone obviously has, because she's asked for you. And it's a big promotion and double the money, and you should be bloody grateful instead of standing there saying why, like a corncrake.

I didn't say anything. Nico sighed. All right, he said. This is just a theory, and I may be completely wrong, but her previous equerry, who had to quit the post on account of being indicted for treason—

You're kidding, I said.

Treason, Nico repeated. Anyhow, he was seventy-two and bald and only had three teeth. I fancy her majesty would like something a bit prettier to look at.

I'm not sure I like the sound of that, I said.

Nico wasn't happy. Who gives a damn what you like or don't like, he said. You've got your orders. Do you want to make trouble for me?

THIS MAY TAKE some explaining, and it's not something I'm comfortable talking about, but here goes. At that point in my life—well, think about it. Use your imagination. Back home in the village, everybody reckoned we were the plague, and you don't get to meet girls that way. Then we were thieves, in Chastel and Roches, doing our level best to be completely invisible. Also, to be absolutely honest with you, it wasn't something I was, well, all that interested in. I think to a certain extent it was about Nico, what he'd done to himself; and what my mother had been, and what people thought about her because of that. All in all, that stuff only made people unhappy and led to a lot of trouble.

Edax didn't think so; but he's always looked quite a lot like a rat, so what he got in that line he mostly had to pay for, and generally speaking we couldn't afford it.

So—what Nico said, what you've never had you don't miss. Also I was awkward about how I looked, guilty even, as though I'd been given more than my fair share—and it wasn't something I could hide, it was like a rich man's kid sent to work down at the docks, kitted out in twenty-thaler shoes and a silk shirt. I felt ridiculous, a walking contradiction; because it says in Scripture, the beautiful is good and the good is beautiful. Anyway, you get the general idea.

With an attitude like that, you won't be surprised to learn that I hadn't had very much to do with women generally, apart from my mother, who doesn't count. They scared me; partly the way men scared me, because I was afraid they were going to throw stones at me or hit me with a stick, partly because I was worried they might like what they saw and want it. I'm not excusing any of this, incidentally, I'm not asking you to forgive me or say that I was right, or anything other than a mess. I've always had a thing about not being touched. It makes me feel sick.

THE EMPRESS BIA lived in the North Tower, everybody knew that. You can see the North Tower from practically anywhere in the City, because it's so very tall. People liked that. They felt safe because the old emperor's daughter was watching over them, they said.

It takes a very long time to walk up all those stairs. It's one of those horrible spiral staircases, with nothing to hold on to, and if you meet someone coming up when you're coming down, both of you are screwed. By the time you get to the top, your knees have turned to jelly and you get splints in your shins enough to make you burst into tears.

Her majesty's apartment was the whole of the top floor. It was huge. There were no walls dividing it up; there in the far distance was the Imperial bed, hung round with curtains, and all the rest of it was a tumultuous sea of cushions, with benches, like in a carpenter's shop, all round the walls. All the benches were crowded out with bottles and jars and iron stands fitted with clamps, and there were these little charcoal stoves under tripods, with pans and glass jars bubbling away. The place stank of roses and violets and honeysuckle, and there was a thick bank of fog about two feet thick directly under the ceiling.

There was no door at the top of the stairs, so I just walked in and there I was. And there she was, bending over the bench, looking at me over her shoulder. Who the hell are you, she said.

I explained. She looked at me. Well, don't just stand there, she said. Come over here and make yourself useful.

Things never seem to turn out the way I expect them to. I never imagined I'd ever be useful. I never thought I'd learn the perfume trade. I never thought I'd fall in love with an old woman, or an empress. Come to that, I never expected my prayers would be answered, ever.

She taught me the perfume trade, which was the first useful thing I'd ever learned in my life. You make perfume by crushing, infusing, distilling and compounding. It involves a lot of hard, repetitive work, grinding stuff in a mortar, and a lot of standing around holding things steady over a flame, and an awful lot of washing out bottles. I enjoyed it. The empress said I was good at it, which pleased me a lot. She talked to me—mostly things like hold this, do that, no, you're doing that all wrong, but sometimes explaining why this added to this was so much more than just the sum of its parts, and why that essence added to that oil worked, and that added to that didn't. It was as though she'd known me all her life, and we were just two people working together.

And she was beautiful. Her hair was dyed—she told me the ingredients and how to mix them, and why she used this rather than that—and there were crow's feet round her eyes and the backs of her hands were all veins, but she was the most beautiful woman I'd ever stood close to. Her arms were long, a bit skinny, with muscles like a man's, but she shaved off all the hair (I'd heard of that but never seen it before). She had about two dozen porcelain jars full of stuff she put on her face and arms, and the edges of her eyes were traced round with a sort of blue pencil.

Nico sent for me. By now I was used to long walks and long staircases. You're looking good, Nico said. How's it going?

I told him I was happy and doing well. He looked at me as though I was talking a foreign language. How's it going, he repeated. Come on, don't be all shy, I'm your brother.

I just told you, I said.

He looked at me like I was simple. The old woman, he said. Has she jumped you yet?

SHE'D TOLD ME about her life; not a single, sustained narrative, just little scraps here and there, which I'd stuck together like the bits of a broken pot. When she was a girl, she was given to understand that she was sitting on a golden throne on top of a very high mountain, and all the world was at her feet, and that was exactly how it should be. One day, they told her, her prince would come; but not just any prince, oh no. Actually, her prince wouldn't be a prince. For her to marry into the ruling house of another nation would be to imply that that nation was equal in stature with the Empire, which was utterly ridiculous. So, her prince would be an Imperial subject, but that was all right; and he'd be a member of one of the twenty or so great and honourable families, but no problem there. And she wouldn't be able to marry until his imperial majesty Daddy had given her a baby brother; well, that was all right too, because Daddy was trying really, really hard on that score, and what Daddy set his mind to do, Daddy did.

(She saw him, she said, on average twice a month—when he wasn't away at the wars, which was actually most of the time. Nurse and a small army of handmaidens would take her through the corridors, under all the mosaic ceilings and past all the gilded murals, to a little room with plain whitewashed walls, where Daddy went to sit when he wasn't on duty. She remembered him as a short man with a mostly bald head burnt brown by the sun, looking up at her from a jumble of papers, which he'd be staring at through a thick circle of glass on a golden stick. He'd look at her as though he'd never seen anything like her in his life, then smile, and ask her some questions about things he obviously wasn't interested in, and then she could go. She was a bit scared of him but she quite liked him, because he looked so funny.)

But there was no baby brother. So she waited, spending the time improving her already perfect self. She learned all the languages that ever there were, read all the books, studied music (stringed instruments, because blowing into a tube isn't ladylike). She was taught how to glide rather than walk, the exactly ideal way of sitting, back and neck straight, chin at precisely ninety degrees to the horizontal, checked from time to time with a set square. She learned to be witty without being insufferable, and how to be bored to death without showing it.

The longer she had to wait, the more lessons she had time for, therefore the more perfect she got. And she knew she was the most beautiful woman in the world, because everyone told her so, and she believed them because her father was Daddy, brother of the Invincible Sun, so it was just common sense, really. And she waited, growing steadily more perfect, like a stalactite built up by drips; and still no baby brother, and time was getting on. There's plenty of time, her maids and tutors told her; but they were starting to sound worried when they said it, and maybe (it occurred to her for the first time) perfection isn't something you can hold on to for ever. True, with every day that passed she was getting more fascinating and brilliant, but now her maids were taking longer and longer to do her face, and there were all these creams and ointments for her skin, and then she noticed her first grey hair, and then a few more.

Now she'd started looking at boys around the age when girls do that sort of thing; but she knew who she was, and it wouldn't do to burn the poor creatures up with her unattainable radiance, now would it? One of her tutors had a serious talk with her when she was fifteen. Think of the Empire, he said, and there'll be plenty of time for all that later. And day followed day, and every day was pretty much the same. She was content to drift, she said, because she had faith. She had faith in God, and Daddy was God's brother, it said so on the backs of the coins.

And then she stopped looking in mirrors, and took up perfume-making instead. It came, she said, as a complete revelation to her. Something she could do, and do well. I knew how she must have felt, I told her, and she looked at me.

Then Daddy died, and suddenly everything was different. She was the princess again, and everything depended on her. She could come down out of the Tower now, if she wanted. She could do anything she chose. She could marry that nice boy she'd noticed, a few years back.

She'd been looking forward to it, she told me, for twenty years, and when it happened, it was horrible. Partly the disappointment. She'd imagined what it must feel like, over and over again; like it feels when you use your finger, she reasoned, only so much better. Instead, she told me, she panicked, and started yelling; keep your voice down, he'd hissed at her, they'll think you're being murdered. So; back to square one. But she remembered that she was Daddy's daughter, and you keep trying, and you never give up, no matter what. And then, she told me, suddenly it was wonderful, and she loved her handsome husband, and she couldn't stop thinking about it, every minute, every day. True, it didn't seem to be having the desired effect. But that only made him try harder—like Daddy, presumably—and she didn't mind that at all.

And then, one morning, she woke up to find maids and equerries packing her clothes and pots and hairbrushes into big wicker baskets. What's going on, she asked, and they told her, she was being moved, back to the North Tower. She was furious about that, but it turned out that there was nothing she could do—which came as a bit of a surprise, since she'd been under the impression that she was the Emperor's daughter and niece of the Invincible Sun, but apparently not.

Since then—Do what you like, he'd written to her, (written, mind you; maybe all those stairs were too much for him, at his age) so long as you don't make trouble and don't leave the Tower. So she lit her little stoves and sent out for herbs and oils, and she created the post of principal equerry to the Empress. Five or six of them had come and gone, and nobody seemed to care what a barren old woman got up to at the top of a tower, and she realised she simply wasn't interested any more. So she got rid of the handsome young men and appointed an old one who knew a bit about alchemy. But he didn't have much conversation and his eyes were bad so he started knocking over bottles, and then there was me.

You arranged it, I said. You fixed it because you wanted her to—

Well yes, Nico said, surprised by my stupidity, of course I did. Catnip to a cat.

Why? I asked him.

You keep asking me that, said my brother. It's obvious, isn't it? You're going to be the next emperor.

So I went to the empress and told her everything.

Not sure what I expected to happen. Most likely, she'd send for the guards and have me and my brothers executed. Or she'd look at me like I was something she'd walked in on the sole of her shoe. Or she'd start crying, or yelling. She looked at me. Why not, she said.

It would be relatively easy, she told me. She'd been giving it serious thought, on and off, for some time, and she knew how it could be done. The problem had always been finding someone to help her.

Last time she'd seen the Emperor, he was pretty fit and hearty for a man of his age. But old men have weak hearts, everyone knows that; and old men don't listen to their doctors, who tell them to take it easy, not eat this, lay off on that. The Emperor liked to take a morning swim in the big indoor pool, heated by underground hypocausts, he'd had built in the South Wing. He'd splash up and down, revelling in the freedom from his steadily increasing weight. And generally he was alone, with guards no closer than the doors outside.

She showed me how to brew foxglove flowers to extract the medicinal essence. Useful, she said, because it stimulates the heart if it should happen to stop; a life-saver. But you know what they say about too much of a good thing.

When I told Nico I'd do it, he laughed. Of course you will, he told me, you're a good boy, and it's the only way we can be absolutely safe. I'm not doing it for you, I told him. Don't talk stupid, he said, of course you are. He didn't believe me. I don't know why.

There was a lot of planning involved; Nico saw to it, of course. The problem, he said, was who we could trust. He had people who'd do anything he told them without a moment's thought, but he didn't trust them further than he could spit. Which left the three of us. And Edax—we looked at each other and decided, no. All right then, Nico said, it's you and me. And everybody in the palace knows me, so you'll have to do quite a bit of the actual running about.

First, he had me reassigned back to the Emperor. That wasn't hard for people to believe, since people said Her Majesty used up her pretty young men quite fast (people say a lot of things, don't they?) After I'd been there a few days, the Cupbearer General had a terrible accident. A loose tile fell on his head, and he died. There was a vacancy for a new cupbearer. I got it.

Nico, I said to him, what the hell did you have to go and do that for? He told me it really was an accident; the tile was meant to break his collar bone, but the man I used was a fool, it's so hard to get good help these days. I believed him, or I chose to believe him. Next time, I said, for crying out loud hire someone competent. There won't be a next time, he said. We're nearly there now, home and dry.

(On one condition, she'd said.)

I looked at her. What?

She looked at me back, then did one of those oh-for-crying-out-loud sighs that women seem to specialise in. All right, fine, she said. In years to come, how do you think the history books will describe us?

That wasn't something I wanted to think about. Murderers, I said. Traitors. The most evil man and woman who ever lived.

She shook her head. They'll say, the empress and her lover. But you aren't, are you? Not yet.

Like I said, I have this problem with physical contact. I like you a lot, I said, more than any woman I've ever known. More than any man, come to that, outside of my family. But—

It's the deal, she said. Either we're in this together, or we aren't.

(By that point, it was too late to back out. Nico had told me that, when I'd asked him, the day before, if we couldn't just forget about the whole thing. We can't, he said. Why not? You and your damned questions, he said. Because I've started Cratylus on a course of slow poison—I couldn't use a quick one, he's got a food-taster—and when he dies, not if, when, all hell is going to break loose. And if by then you're not the emperor, we're all three of us dead. Capisce?)

We're in this together, I said, I promise you.

Well then, she said.

When all else fails, be honest with the people you love. And I did love her, at that moment, under those circumstances, on that anvil. I've never done it before, I said.

You're kidding, she said; and then, Oh well. Late starters, both of us. But you'll soon catch up.

It was awkward, the first time. She told me what I had to do, and I remember saying, Are you sure? And she gave me a look that would've killed slugs. Yes, she said. Actually, the first few times were a mess. But after that; after that, I fell head over heels in love with her. Still am, to this day.

THE FOXGLOVE POWDER was in a little bottle, which she gave me. I took it down to the Stables and showed it to Nico. He unstoppered it and gave it a sniff. That's the good stuff, he said. She really made it herself?

I nodded.

She's a clever lady, Nico said. Then he pulled a ring off his finger. It was a big, broad ring with a fat stone. I hadn't seen him wearing it before. He didn't do jewellery, or any of that stuff. Watch carefully, he said, and did something I couldn't see, and the stone popped out and hinged back. Plenty of space in there for six grains, he said, which is all it'll take.

He made me put the ring on, and practice flipping the tiny catch till I could do it without looking down. Then he filled it with powder and snapped it shut. Be careful, he said. That's nasty stuff you've got there.

Are you sure that'll be enough? I asked.

Trust me, he said. I'm your brother.

IT HAD TO be done, Nico had told me; because the Guardian had been out to get him for a long time, ever since he'd risen to Count of the Stables. Why? Because the Guardian was afraid of him, the same way the rabbit is afraid of the fox, and so he'd resolved to kill him or disgrace him, preferably both—that's how the Service works, Nico told me, predators and prey. He'll destroy me unless I destroy him first. And if I go, so will you, and Edax. And all of this has been about you, right from the start. And then he got impatient with me. Come on, he said, it's the last step, and then we'll be safe. We've come so far, ever such a long way from the village, and if we stop now we're all dead men. He looked at me. Is that what you want? Nico said. Do you want to see me and Edax flayed alive in the Square and our heads on pikes? No, sorry, you won't see that, because your head'll be up there too. Is that really what you want?

IT WAS HIS heart, the doctors said, though the immediate cause of death was drowning. He'd been found floating face down in his private pool, the one I told you about. There was nothing anyone could have done. It was his own fault, the doctors told her privately. He ate too much of the wrong sort of food, never took any exercise, it was simply a matter of time. He could have gone at any moment over the last two years.

I was waiting at the foot of the North Tower stairs when she came down. We both knew exactly what had to be done. Nico had made me repeat it, over and over again till I knew it by heart; I'd told her and she didn't need any of it repeated. We were to go directly to the Purple Chamber, not stopping, not saying a word to anybody. There would be a company of guards waiting for us outside the Tower, in the little quad; if anyone tried to stop us, their orders were to use their swords, flats for choice but edges if needs be. But that shouldn't happen, because Nico had called a meeting in the Ivory Chapter, to announce the death of the Guardian of the Orphans. So we ought to have the place to ourselves, he said, and he was right.

We got to the Purple, and there was the abbot of the Studium, with the precentor and a half-dozen other priests I didn't recognise. First we were married, and then she sat me down on the throne and put the crown on my head and the lorus round my shoulders. Then she sat down beside me, with her own crown and lorus; I got the sceptre and globe cruciger, and the Sword of State across my knees, while she got the labarum and the golden acacia. And that, Nico had assured us, was all we had to do. Just leave the rest to him.

So we sat and waited, and the distinguished clergymen stood about, because there didn't seem to be any chairs for them. Sweat was running down my face in streams, but she just sat there with a sort of faraway look in her eyes; and I remember thinking; in my dream it was Edax instead of her, but of course I didn't know her back then. And otherwise, it's pretty much the same. This is why, the dream said. After about ten minutes of just sitting, she carefully put down the labarum (still looking straight ahead, not at me) and took the globe off me and put it down somewhere, and took my hand and gave it a little squeeze.

Then the doors flew open, and I remember feeling the sort of sharp stitch in my guts that you tend to get when you've eaten too much fried food. And all these men came in; men in black robes, and soldiers in armour. I looked for Nico but I couldn't see him. Oh well, I thought, and I'd have prayed, only there wasn't time.

Then a side door I hadn't realised was there opened, and in came Nico. He was wearing this ridiculous cloth-of-gold thing that trailed along the ground after him, and there were a dozen steelnecks in full parade armour behind him. And I noticed that they had weapons, and the ones who'd come in earlier didn't. In fact they weren't proper soldiers, just generals and admirals in uniform. And Nico turned to face us, and bowed deeply, and all the people I didn't know followed suit, and that was that, basically.

NICO HAD STITCHED it all together quite beautifully. He'd framed the Guardian by transferring about two million acres of government land into his name, using a whole load of shell corporations and stuff like that; his death was presented to the imperial court as suicide. Found in his cold dead hand was a letter (Nico had a wonderful forger; he had him killed afterwards, just to be safe, but he said it was a dreadful waste) confessing that he'd embezzled public property and been found out by the Count of the Stables—Nico—and fear of arrest and execution had driven him to murder the emperor and empress, using a decoction of foxglove, and seize the throne. But the empress had eluded his clutches, thanks to the interference of her equerry, and he knew the game was up, so he'd taken the easy way out, and may the Invincible Sun have mercy, etcetera.

My part in it all (according to Nico's version, which became the official version, which is by definition the definitive truth) was rather dashing and romantic. I'd grappled with the assassins sent by the Guardian and hurled them from the top of the Tower into the moat below—that was a nice touch, wasn't it?—whereupon the Empress, in an access of magnanimous gratitude, had married me on the spot. Now, there could be absolutely no doubt that she was the old emperor's daughter—the only one available for secular duty, her elder sister being a Bride of the Sun—and therefore by indisputable right the empress. And there was no doubt whatsoever that she'd married me, because here were eight of the leading churchmen in the empire to bear witness. And the empress's husband was the emperor. So simple, even a child could get it. After all, the idiot Apsimar had only been emperor because he was married to Princess Bia, and now he was dead, and she had a new husband. Well, then.

It's because it was done quickly, Nico told me later, and because I pinned everything on the Guardian (Nico was Guardian now, needless to say) and it made people feel like there'd been an attempted coup that failed, rather than an attempted coup that succeeded. Also, the people love her, because of her dad, and they reckon she's been hard done by, and in their minds she's still twenty-one and pretty as a picture, and all the stuff about me fighting off the assassins and her marrying me out of sheer gratitude was pure fairytale and so they loved it. And it doesn't hurt that there's absolutely nobody else, not unless we want a civil war.

THIS IS WHY, said the dream. And you've probably noticed, I have a habit of asking, Why? Used to drive Nico mad; it doesn't matter a flying fuck why, he'd yell at me, just do as you're told; and I did, because he was my big brother and he loved me. Why isn't something you say to those who are bigger and stronger than you are, and who have your destiny in their hands, and who love you without limit or reserve.

Like that story in Scripture—my favourite—where He sends all sorts of affliction down on His most faithful and loving servant; and the servant asks, why? And He says, For reasons you couldn't possibly begin to understand. Where were you when I laid the foundations of the Earth? He says, and what the hell do you know about anything?

Which is a good answer, sure enough, except it's always niggled away at me, like a bit of crab meat stuck between my teeth. And so I keep my speculations to myself, except He can read my mind.

But He'd been good enough to explain, though, hadn't He? This is why; clear as daylight, except it was in a dream. But I don't ever remember my dreams when I wake up, and I remembered that one. This is why. And I'd started it, by praying to Him, twice, and twice He'd answered me, and rescued me out of the hands of my enemies. True, there's Nico's point. But all that goes to prove is that He made the messes that He later got me out of. Why? Why indeed. And what the hell do I know about anything?

This is why. He put me on the imperial throne—me, the last person in the world to expect or deserve it—and therefore He had to have a reason. I wasn't entirely sure I understood, but that didn't matter. I'm too stupid to understand, I accept that. I don't understand trigonometry either, but I have absolutely no doubt that it's valid and true. I believed. I trusted. I had no choice but to believe and trust, because it was as plain as the nose on my face.

He'd put me there; not, obviously, as an end in itself, but as a beginning. I was there to do a job. For that job, he'd chosen me, just as Nico chose me to be Apsimar's cupbearer. So, what was it about me that made me the right man for the job? Think about that.

I had no ambition to be emperor. The pleasures of the flesh, for want of a better word, had never meant much to me (what you've never had, you don't miss). Most of all, I knew that He existed and had put me there to do the job that He wanted. As far as any mortal man could be, I was empty of any kind of selfish thought or motive—

Well, not quite. But I'd have to be.

I loved my wife, and I loved my brother. And both of them were murderers, traitors, regicides. Me too, of course. But He hadn't chosen them to be his instrument.

It won't come to that, I thought. And then I dropped to my knees and clasped my hands together so tight my fingers hurt, and I prayed; Don't make it come to that.

BIA AND I stayed in the throne room for the rest of the day, mostly because we couldn't be sure it was safe anywhere else. Then Nico came back and told us to go to bed. Fortunately she remembered the way.

The royal bedchamber was smaller than I'd expected; very plain, almost dingy. It used to be Daddy's room, she explained, and when Apsimar wanted to change it she'd thrown a dozen fits, and he'd given in to stop her making a scene. When he'd banished her back to her tower he'd moved to the apartments in the Pearl Cloister, with his mistress du jour. He couldn't fuck properly in the old emperor's room, he used to say, he always felt like the old devil was in there, looking down on him and scowling.

She sat down on the bed and took her shoes off. They'd been killing her all day, she said. I found a chair—there were two in the room—and sat down opposite. What now, I said.

I don't know, she answered. I guess it's all up to that clever brother of yours.

I took a deep breath. I want to be a good emperor, I said.

She looked at me as if I was mad. Is that right?

Yes, I said. Nico says Apsimar was a bad emperor. He says he's ruined the economy and wasted huge amounts of money, and the farmers can't afford to pay their taxes, and there are thousands of people starving in the City because of the corn monopolies, and the Robur are going to attack because he stopped paying the tribute. He says unless something's done, the empire will fall.

She shrugged. I don't know much about politics, she said. But I think people always say that sort of thing. And sometimes it's true and sometimes it isn't. And you never know which it is at the time, because everything always looks the same. At least, it does in the palace.

Nico should know, I said. And he told me things are very bad.

She didn't look particularly interested. You be a good emperor, then, she said, if that's what you'd like.

I'm serious, I said. She gave me one of her looks. You clown, she said. It's not up to you. You're just—and she stopped. What? I asked her. Never mind, she said. Look, why don't you just leave everything to your brother? He's a smart man, anyone can see that. He wouldn't have got where he is today if he wasn't the smartest man in the empire.

Then Nico came in, without knocking, and sat down on the bed, right next to her. That went off all right, he said, you both did very well. Now, listen carefully, I haven't got much time.

And he told us what we had to do, which wasn't very much; show yourselves in the throne room immediately after Matins, stay there till noon, then ride in an open carriage to the White Shell temple for Low Mass, then down to the Arsenal to bless the new flagship of the fleet, then back to the throne room for afternoon petitions; here's what you have to do about those—and he gave Bia a piece of paper. He can't read, he told her, but that's all right, just give him a nudge, once for yes, twice for no. Then there's a reception for the Mysian ambassador, which is basically just sitting still and looking royal, then dinner and the rest of the day's your own.

You've got to get rid of her, Nico said.

I'd avoided being alone with him, but he knew the palace routine. He knew, for example, that her majesty took a bath, in asses' milk and honey, at a certain time every other day, and I couldn't very well follow her in there, because she didn't like me watching while she was patched up and maintained, which took a long time and a large staff.

No, I said. I love her.

He had that look on his face. No, he said, you don't. And besides, it's ruining everything.

I don't understand, I told him.

He sighed. You look ridiculous, he said. A young man, not much more than a boy, and an old woman, holding hands, in public. People are starting to make jokes about it.

I didn't understand. You told me she was really popular. You said the people love her.

Yes, but they hadn't seen her for years. Now they can see she's got old. They're making all sorts of dirty cracks about the two of you, and it's really bad for morale. Also, it's obvious she's far too old to have a kid, which sets people thinking. She's got to go.

I felt cold all over. No, I said.

Don't be stupid, he said. You can't divorce her, obviously, and while she's alive you can't marry and have a legitimate heir. Tell you what, he went on, as though he was doing me a tremendous favour, we'll pretend she's dead, and that'll be just as good. We can have a grand state funeral, mother of her country and all that, and then she can stay up in her tower, you can marry and breed and we'll be safe. A stable, guaranteed succession is the only way to ensure stability, everyone knows that. You needn't kill her if that'd upset you, but she's got to go.

I THOUGHT ABOUT how I was going to do it for a long time. I'd never done anything like it before—Nico had always seen to everything like that—and if I got it wrong there'd be hell to pay. But I was a complete novice, a virgin. Not a clue.

So I got into the habit of an hour or so alone in the evenings, between dinner and bed. I told Nico I was having a course of massage, which made him smirk, and I told Bia I was learning to read, which she approved of. And I found myself a clerk.

I came across him quite by chance. I'd got lost—something that happened painfully often in that place—and I wandered into some office or other, where there were half a dozen clerks on tall stools, copying things out. One of them, I noticed, was a brown man; not a common sight. I only noticed him because he looked different. All the other clerks in the Service are indistinguishable.

You, I said. Come with me.

He looked worried. I'm not supposed to leave my desk, he said. I'm the emperor, I told him. Do as you're told.

So I had a quiet time, a place to go (I found a little room everyone seemed to have forgotten about and nobody ever used) and a clerk. I told him, go to the library and get me a book about government.

He gave me a terrified look.

Get me, I said, a book about how you run an empire. There's got to be one. Bring it here and read it to me.

He must've thought I was mad, but away he went, and some time later he came back with a big book, which turned out to be *Institutions of the Imperial Court*, written a hundred years ago by the old emperor's grandfather. That sounded promising. Read it to me, I told him.

I lasted about five minutes, then stopped him. That's no good, I said.

Majesty?

That's all useless, I said, it's ceremonial and protocol, and who has precedence at levees and lyings in state. Skip all that.

So he flipped though the pages, most of the book, until there was only about a finger's breadth left. Then he started reading again; and it was the good stuff. Sources of revenue, organisation of the provincial governments, chains of command in the military, the structure and function of the civil service. He read for about an hour, and then there wasn't any more to read.

You're Robur, aren't you? I asked him

He looked nervous. I used to be, majesty, but I'm a citizen now. I love the empire.

What's your name, I asked him.

Gemellus Constantianus, he said. I shook my head. Your real name, I said. What your mother called you.

I'd asked him something personal and embarrassing, which he was ashamed about. My Robur name, he said, was Heaven Thunders The Truth.

I raised my eyebrows. That's a name?

Where I came from, our majesty.

I can't call you that, I said. All right, say it in Robur.

So he said something, and I only caught the first bit of it, because it was just noises. Would it be all right, I said, if I call you Bemba, for short?

As your majesty pleases, he said.

Bemba was a short man, he just about came up to my shoulder; about fifty years old, bald as an egg, only a faint trace of an accent; he'd been sold to the Service thirty-six years ago, after he was stolen from his family by traders, and the City was his home now, and the Service was his life. And now, having read me the book, he knew as much about running the empire as I did, and probably more. Well, you've got to start somewhere.

Why haven't you got rid of her yet? Nico kept asking me. I'm scared, I told him. What if it goes wrong? You're useless, he said, I'll do it. Just leave everything to me. You won't hurt her, I asked him, will you? And he looked at me as if I'd just wet myself. No, of course not, he said. You're my brother. Would I ever do anything that'd upset you?

THANKS TO BEMBA and the book I was beginning to understand who ran the empire. The emperor, obviously; except the empire is huge, so one man can't do all that, even if he's God's brother, so naturally he delegates; and over the years, everything had been delegated. Most of everything was done by the Service, which was run by two senior officials, the Guardian of the Orphans and the Count of the Stables. The Count was in charge of three of the five departments, but the Guardian had the two that mattered; war and the treasury. Now, of course, Nico was both the Count and the Guardian, which meant he had everything.

But not quite. The army had its own traditions. For centuries, it had chosen its leaders from six families, who between them owned about a quarter of the land in the empire, and naturally enough they hated the Service and the Service loathed them. Money to pay the troops came from the treasury via the war office, which was how the Service kept the army commanders under control; also, it was a long-standing rule that no military units were to be stationed within two hundred miles of the City (apart from the palace guard, which was under the command of the Count of the Stables) and any general who came within that distance without first resigning his command was automatically a traitor and sentenced to death.

The old emperor had spent more time with the army than in the City, and he'd been a good commander. Apsimar didn't like soldiers and was scared stiff of the generals; also, he wanted money for the university he'd founded, and it pained him to think of the soldiers getting paid for just sitting around, so he'd dissolved two of the eight field armies, the two which happened to be commanded by the Stilian brothers, members of the oldest and proudest of the six army families. With no soldiers to lead, he figured, they couldn't be a threat to anyone, now could they?

Bemba wrote a letter to Stilian Zautzes, asking him to come to the City as soon as he possibly could, and sealed it with my private seal, which Nico had carelessly left lying about in a locked desk (I owed Bemba a dukedom for that; if they'd caught him, he'd have been crucified) Now, chances were, Stilian would think it was a trap, and a pretty crude one at that. But he had reason to feel safe in the City, even if it was. The palace guard, about eight thousand strong, was recruited from the very best men in the field armies; it was a sort of pension for fifteen years plus of exemplary service. And Stilian's army had been the best in the empire (before Apsimar dissolved it), so half the men in the guard were his veterans, and they worshipped him. The letter hadn't gone into detail—too risky; we only dared send it because Bemba found out there was one other Robur clerk—just one—in the domestic Service, and he was in the Postmaster's office, and could get away and deliver it without anyone taking much notice—but Bemba had chosen his words well, with the lines artfully spaced for reading between. So Stilian came; and Bemba let him in at the back door of the kitchen and brought him to see me.

He didn't like me, not one bit, I could tell. I was too pretty, for one thing, and my clothes stank of Bia's perfumes, and he didn't approve of an old woman' gigolo being emperor, even though he'd thought Apsimar was the devil incarnate. I rather liked Stilian. He was short and stocky, grey haired and grey eyed, and he had that accent that only army officers have, which I must admit I quite like. Anyway, I told him what I had in mind and what I wanted him to do. He looked at me as if I was mad. Can't be done, he said. And if they catch us, they'll cut my head off. I felt like I was about to piss down my leg I was so scared, but I looked straight at him. If we don't do it now, I said, we won't get another chance. You do want what's best for the empire, don't you?

You're either mad or very stupid, he said. What's that got to do with anything? I asked.

I WASN'T THERE to see it, of course. I was in our bedroom when it happened, in the middle of the night, which is always the best time for anything like that. But Bemba went along, to be my witness and to carry the Great Seal in case anyone needed to see it.

Later, Stilian told me the story. He'd had no trouble finding the men. He'd chosen a dozen of his old NCOs, men who'd served under him in the old emperor's time; he told them to meet him in the quad next to the South Cloister at the start of Prime, and sure enough, there they were. They made their way quickly and quietly through the corridors, with Bemba leading the way, until they reached Nico's room. The door wasn't even locked. He was sitting up in bed reading official papers. They didn't give him time to say a word, according to Stilian. They stuffed his mouth with rags, tied his hands and hustled him out of there in his nightshirt and bare feet.

They didn't have far to go; about a hundred yards to the kitchen gate, where Bemba had let Stilian in, and then a quarter of a mile through empty streets to the Golden Shell temple. One of the canons there owed Stilian's cousin a large sum of money, so there was no trouble; doors unlocked, everything they needed laid out ready for them. They tied Nico to a prebendary stall, shaved his head so he'd be acceptable as a monk, and put his eyes out. It's an old-established tradition, so they tell me, in the Imperial court; it effectively gets rid of someone as a potential threat without actually killing them, which is why it's referred to as the Divine Clemency of the Emperor. I wish they hadn't told me that.

From there, he was taken by boat down the South canal to the harbour, where Stilian had arranged passage (you can see why he was such a good general) for Nico and three guards to the Blue Rock monastery on the island of Olethria. In case you haven't heard of it, it's a rock in the middle of the sea—sailors know how to find it, apparently, but it's not on any maps.

She stared at me when I told her. What the hell did you do that for, she said.

I told her. She went white as a sheet. He wanted me to have you killed, I told her, so I could marry someone else and have kids, for the succession.

I want him dead, she said. Right now.

He's my brother, I told her. And he did it all for me, and Edax. Then I realised. She hadn't known Nico was my brother. She'd figured out that we knew each other, that Nico had arranged for me to be assigned to her because I was good-looking, but that was as far as she'd got; and I assumed she knew, and besides, I never really talked much about myself. It doesn't matter, I told her. He had to go anyway, for the empire.

She scowled at me. What are you talking about, she said.

For the empire, I said. He'd never have let me put anything right. He wasn't interested in that sort of thing. He only cared about getting power and holding on to it—so we'd be all right, him and me and our kid brother Edax. He'd have told me not to be so bloody stupid, and leave everything to him, and keep out of things that don't concern me. And when he got rid of the old Guardian, he took all that embezzled land for himself, and I know he'd never have given it back, and we'll need that money. He'd have said it was for just-in-case; in case anything went wrong and we had to clear out in a hurry and go somewhere else. He's very careful, my brother, he always expects the worst.

(Except he hadn't; not the very worst. But nobody's perfect.)

She looked at me as though I was a stranger. Well, she said, it's done now. And nobody liked him anyway.

I APPOINTED GENERAL Stilian as the new Guardian. It had never been done before, having a soldier in charge of the war office, not to mention everything else. I had no idea whether I could trust him or not, and I was well aware he didn't like me, but I didn't see that I had any choice. I didn't know anyone else.

And I made Bemba the new Count. I figured, he has no friends, nobody's ever wanted him on their side, nobody's spoken to him unless they absolutely had to, but he knows his way round the Service; he'll be on my side, because he'll know that if anything happens to me, he'll be dead within the hour. That's how you make sure of loyalty. Love and trust don't work, I've found.

First thing I had them do was make a list of everything that was wrong with the empire. It sounds stupid, doesn't it, but I thought, we might as well start at the beginning.

It was worse than I thought; worse, I think, than anyone had realised, even Nico, who was so smart. To start with, all the money had gone. When the old emperor died, we'd had a surplus of something like twelve billion; now we owed something like seven billion to the banks and the merchant venturers, and we didn't dare default because it'd start a panic and everything would go to hell. We couldn't raise taxes, because taxes were too high already. The way it works is, the treasury fixes on an amount for each province and charges it to the districts, who pass the assessments on to the landowners, who pass it on to the tenants, with a little bit extra added for luck at each stage. Things were so bad that farmers were simply packing up and leaving, without any clear idea of where they were going, and large parts of the eastern and southern provinces—where all the grain for the City comes from—were just empty houses and fields full of briars and nettles. A fair number of them ended up in the City, where they thought they might find work, but taxes were high there, too, and workshops and factories were going out of business every day. The price of grain in the City had doubled over the last six months, and rather too often there simply wasn't any grain to buy, not at any price, because the corn-chandlers were in debt to the merchant venturers, who had a habit of sequestering the grain barges before they reached the City harbour and sending them off to Scheria or Messagene, where prices (because of the strength of the Scherian angel and the Messagene thaler against the Imperial solidus) were higher.

None of which bothered general Stilian particularly, since his family estates were in the north, and the City could burn to the ground for all he cared. What really upset him was the fact that the peasant farmers and smallholders whose sons had supplied the army with recruits for a thousand years were being driven off the land by the thousand, when the rich City aristocrats called in their mortgages, so they could take the land and work it with slave labour. That and Apsimar's dissolution of three regiments meant that the army had shrunk to a third of what it had been in the old emperor's time. But we're at peace, who is there left to fight? Apsimar had said to him, with that winning smile of his, and hadn't waited for an answer.

Besides, Stilian told me, even if you really feel the need to make things better for people, as you put it, you can't, the Service won't let you. I said that the old emperor hadn't allowed the Service to interfere; that made him roar with laughter. The Service is three times bigger than it was in his day, he told me; and I had Bemba look into it, and he was right. Also, its budget was four times what it had been in Basiliscus' day, and ninety per cent of that went on wages, although the pay of the junior grades, three quarters of the total staff, who do the actual work, had fallen by fifteen per cent.

I've never done an honest day's work in my life, so I don't know how it feels. But I can use my imagination. I picture myself walking up from the house to the barn just when the sun rises. I can see myself walking the oxen into the yoke, linking up the plough, driving the team to the field, leaning on the plough-handles to dig the share into the earth as the oxen lurch forward. I can see myself stopping at the end of each furrow to wipe the sweat off my face and look back at what I've done and what I've still got to do. It'll never happen, of course, but I can imagine it.

The field I had to plough in real life was a bit more daunting; and I didn't know how to go about it, or where to start. My plough-oxen, God forgive me for calling them that, were an ill-matched pair. One of them despised me, and the other one was scared stiff of more or less everything; and one was a blue-blood military aristocrat, with a better pedigree than God, and the other one had been born in a Robur caravan and weaned on broth boiled down from the bones of his father's enemies—did I mention the Robur are cannibals? But there; I don't suppose either of them ever thought they'd be serving an emperor whose mother was a village whore. Things don't ever seem to turn out the way we thought they would, but here we all still are. For now, anyway.

I asked Stilian to have a word with the bankers. He scowled at me, but I think the idea appealed to him; his family had lost about a hundred thousand acres to the banks over the last fifty years. He came back and told me that they'd agreed to accept forty nummi on the solidus, with payments spread out over fifty years, at two per cent (we'd been paying five). I have no idea what he said to them, which is probably just as well.

Bemba wrote me a report on the Service. It was very long, carefully copied out on new parchment and rolled up in a gold tube. I pointed out that I couldn't read it, so he read it to me. We put our heads together and decided what to do. The next day, Stilian's guards arrested all twelve heads of department on charges of embezzlement, peculation, dereliction of duty and fraud; the charges would be dropped, Bemba told them, if they cut their departmental budgets by a half and got rid of a third of their staff. Since the penalty for embezzlement in public office is crucifixion, they agreed to see what they could do.

It took a lot of work, ingenuity and imagination to unravel the paper trail Nico had left to cover his ownership of the public land he'd taken over from his predecessor. When we finally got to the bottom of it, we were stunned. A million acres, and none of your rubbish; prime arable in the most fertile districts of the home provinces. We parcelled it up, ten acres a man for a hundred thousand homeless farmers—freehold, I insisted on that, though Stilian called me all the names under the Sun and even Bemba frowned and asked me if I was sure that was a good idea. But it had to be freehold; no rent, no debt. The proviso was, the land couldn't be sold or mortgaged for fifty years. That was for Stilian, and he eventually got the point. A new generation of soldiers for the empire.

Bemba did a bit of digging, and found out that the merchant venturers who held the debt on the corn chandlers' barges had neglected to pay any tax for the last eight years; they'd paid about a quarter of what they owed to Nico's predecessor, and their tax demands somehow got lost in the paperwork. I set Stilian on them—he was starting to enjoy bullying civilians, and I like people to be happy in their work—and we got possession of the barges, which meant we could guarantee supply. We also managed to bring the price down twelve per cent, by cutting costs; not nearly as much as I'd have liked, but at least it was a start. In the medium term, corn would be cheaper, once the newly-installed smallholders started producing and selling; I had Bemba set up a co-operative to buy their grain and sell it to the chandlers at an honest price, though how long that'll last remains to be seen.

Apsimar had commissioned a whole lot of building work—temples, his precious university and a whole new palace (we've already got four palaces in the City). I cancelled all that, but the contractors didn't lose out. Instead, I set them to work renovating the walls—they hadn't been looked at since the old emperor was a boy, and large parts of them were a mess—and paving the City streets, which are so bad in places, you can drown in the wheel-ruts if it's been raining heavily. Ridiculous extravagance, Stilian called it, but it made work for about twelve thousand City men who hadn't had any work for a long time, and I paid for it by selling the books from Apsimar's university, or at least suggesting to the bankers that they might care to take them in lieu of cash for their next instalment of interest. I didn't have to make Stilian go along and make the request, I just had Bemba mention his name. They remembered him very well.

I HAD A private chapel on the top of the East tower. It used to be a lookout post for the beacon system, before the mail was set up. It was small and circular, whitewashed walls, with an icon of the Transfiguration—at least until I found out how much it was worth; then I had it sold and made do with just the wall.

I went there every day to pray. Lord, I said, I have sinned. I murdered the Emperor. I let my brother murder other people—I don't know how many, dozens maybe. I can't think of anything worse than what I've done. And You rewarded me with the Empire, and a chance of making life better for Your people, and—I wasn't quite sure what the word meant, but I used it anyway; happiness. Does this mean I'm forgiven?

The thing is, I had no idea. I'd had a dream, once, under difficult circumstances; this is why. And I'd been shown myself, sitting on the throne (but with Edax next to me; that part of it I couldn't figure out), so I'd assumed that He meant me to become Emperor, so I could do what was pleasing in His sight—and I'd assumed that feeding the poor and putting the Empire to rights must be pleasing in His sight, though maybe I'd been jumping to conclusions. But in order to do that, I'd murdered a man, and I'd stood by while Nico murdered probably dozens more; and there was treason and adultery and all those other bad things, and surely that couldn't be His will?

Where was I when He laid the foundations of the earth? Good question.

So I prayed; Lord, if I'm doing the right thing and what I'm doing is pleasing in Your sight, send me a sign. Something so clear, even an idiot like me can understand it.

I REMEMBER THAT day very clearly. It was the day the news reached the City that the Robur had sacked Charnac.

I ASKED BEMBA about the Robur. Were they really cannibals? Well, yes and no. Most of the time they lived on milk, cheese, butter and yoghurt, along with whatever wild fruit they came across as they lumbered in their enormous wagons across the north-eastern plains. But when they fought anyone, assuming they won, they ate the bodies of men they'd killed, and what they didn't eat fresh they salted down, like bacon. And were they really as merciless as people made out? Yes and no, Bemba said. Among themselves they prized justice, honour and mercy; but none of that applied to people who weren't Robur, therefore by definition inferior and not really human. What did they want, I asked him. To be left alone in peace, mostly; except that when they felt their honour had been insulted, it was their highest duty to avenge it. For instance; they didn't care a damn about gold, silver, silks, ivory, all the things we set so much store by in the Empire. To them, it was all just so much junk that took up space in the wagons that could be used for something useful; when the Emperor sent them gold coins, they buried them, with a pile of stones to mark the spot. No risk of them getting stolen, because who in their right mind would want them?

But when a Robur king dies, he's buried with all the prizes he's won in his lifetime; and Robur kings tend to die at frequent intervals, because they're a competitive people. Now the king had just died, but the Emperor had stopped sending gold, so there was nothing to bury him with, and this was the most appalling dishonour. No good sending tribute now, because the damage had been done. Honour would only be satisfied if they took it by force.

Just how much force exactly, I asked, before honour was satisfied? Bemba thought about that and said he didn't know precisely; as much as it took until they felt better, was about as close as he could get. Also, he said, his people had been cooped up in their grazing-lands for many years, ever since the emperors started paying tribute, which meant the Robur could no longer honourably raid the Empire. A whole generation had grown up without the chance to establish their status by fighting, and to the Robur that sort of thing was desperately important. The most likely thing was that they'd set their heart on burning the City itself. Could they do that, I asked him? Oh yes, he said.

So I asked general Stilian, who told me that the old emperor had never fought the Robur, but his grandfather had; four battles, three of which he lost, the fourth one drawn, and that was when the Tribute started. What made them so special he didn't honestly know. The Robur don't have horses; their wagons are drawn by oxen, and they fight on foot, but they're superb archers with the most marvellous composite cane bows; also, they're very big and strong and brave, and they don't seem to care about getting killed. If only it was possible to hire them as mercenaries, he'd have done so like a shot. But they don't use money, and they think fighting for hire is the most disgusting thing a man can do.

I asked him; do we stand a chance against them? He thought for a very long time, and said; yes, because we've got very good cavalry. But it'd mean bringing up the main cavalry forces from the South and the West, as well as the Northern heavy infantry; we only really stand a chance if we hit them in overwhelming force, and like I've been telling you all this time, the army is dangerously under strength.

Never mind about that, I told him. Overwhelming force it is. He shrugged. I can do that, he said, but I'll need money. I'll see about that, I said, not having the faintest idea where it was going to come from. And I'll want my brothers and my uncle Tzimisces as my battalion commanders. Fine, I said. And then he couldn't think of anything else to ask for on the spur of the moment, and I left him to his plan of campaign.

THE NEXT DAY I received a delegation from the Supreme Conclave. It was led by the abbot of the Studium, and the heads of all the City temples were with him. It was imperative, they told me, that I should put away the empress at once. Otherwise, they would have no choice but to close all the temples and pronounce sentence of excommunication on the entire City.

I asked them as respectfully as I could if they'd all gone raving mad. The City takes its religion seriously; excommunication, particularly with the Robur on the warpath, would mean panic, riots, the guards being called in to stop the riots, at least one horrendous massacre—they knew all that, they assured me, but it had to be done. The law was quite clear. They had no choice.

There's always a choice, I told them, and what's this all about anyway? They looked at me, very gravely. There was evidence, they said, that the empress had murdered her husband, the late emperor. As such she was an abomination in His sight, and unless she was removed and confined, He would punish the Empire. Indeed, it could hardly be a coincidence that His scourge had already been set in motion, a point their priests would be sure to make from every pulpit in the City unless I took immediate action.

I can't do that, I said, she's my wife. I love her.

Maybe I was mumbling or something; they didn't seem to have heard me. At once, they said. In fact, we would prefer it if you issued the order in our presence, right now.

You've got it all wrong, I told them. It wasn't her who killed the old man, it was me.

They looked at me as if I was stupid or something. You are the emperor, they said, the emperor can do no wrong. It would be a legal impossibility for you to be guilty of murder. But someone clearly is; and since there are only two parties involved, it has to be her.

Besides, said the archimandrite of the Crooked Horn, lowering his voice just a little, she's lived in that tower most of her life, she's used to it by now. And you're a young man, and the empire needs an heir. And you're quite popular in the City right now, what with all the reforms, you needn't worry on that score. We've got just the formula for annulling the marriage, and then you'll be free.

I didn't answer him. I can't do it, I said.

You must, they said. It's God's will.

SHE DIDN'T GO quietly. I made sure I wasn't anywhere I could hear, but I gather there was a terrible scene. That evening, the abbot of the Studium made an official announcement at evening prayers. There were no riots, but only because Stilian had posted guards on all the street corners. I sent for the abbot and told him, but he shook his head. It's too late now, he said, the annulment has gone through, and besides, you can't go back on your word. If you do, we'll excommunicate you, and that would mean civil war.

Bemba told me that any support I'd had in the City was gone. I was the cunning, contriving usurper who'd seduced the old emperor's daughter, then had her locked up the moment she stopped being useful. They'd never forgive me for that.

I went to my chapel and prayed. Lord, I said, I think I understand. I did what was unpleasing in your sight, and you punished me; first my brother, now my wife. But you sent me a dream, after I'd prayed to you; this is why, you told me. I've tried to do what I thought you wanted. I expect I got that wrong. I get everything wrong, according to Nico.

So what I'd like you to do, if it's perfectly all right, is to punish me, not the City or the Empire. If you punish me, with death or disgrace or anything You like, I'll know I was wrong all along and I'll go quietly, and I won't ask you for anything ever again. But please, if it's all my fault, don't hurt anyone else because of it.

ON THAT UNDERSTANDING, I sealed Stilian's formal commission for the Robur campaign.

He'd taken me at my word and put together the biggest land army ever fielded in the Empire outside of a civil war. He'd brought up the Second and the Fourth from the south, mostly comprising light and heavy cavalry, and the First from the west, with its eight battalions of heavy infantry. I'd found him some money by appealing to the better nature of the abbot of the Studium, who issued a bull for a tithe of all ecclesiastical property in the City; I was stunned by how much that came to, but never mind; that particular gift horse had golden teeth.

We had a big service for him in the Studium chapel, and another in the Offertory, and then off he went. That night I repeated my prayer, just in case He hadn't heard me.

It would be all right, Bemba told me. If there was one thing on earth his people were terrified of, it was men on horses. In the past, when they'd fought us, they'd stuck to the mountains, where cavalry can't go. But now they were down in the plains, with nowhere to hide. Besides, Stilian was a fine general. He'd learned his trade under the old emperor.

Next morning I woke up and found both my ankles had swollen. They were as thick as my calves, and when I pressed them with my thumb, I left a thumb-sized hollow. So I sent for the doctors, who said it was nothing to worry about, and they'd be back the next day. The morning after that, the swelling was up to my thighs. You've got dropsy, the doctors said.

Ah, I thought. So that's all right.

IN THE WEEKS that followed, I drew great strength and satisfaction from my sickness. I don't know if you're familiar with dropsy; you swell up like a wineskin, your skin goes purple, your joints ache horribly all the time and no matter what you do, you can't get comfortable. I couldn't get to my chapel at the top of the tower—I couldn't leave my chair without three men to help me—but I prayed nonetheless. Thank you, I said.

I knew it had to be the answer to my prayers, because it was just the right illness for me to have. All those good looks, all that prettiness, gone. Instead I turned into this ludicrous bloated monster, like an animal that's been dead for a week. My skin was sort of glazed, like ham cured with honey, and it took me all my time and effort just to breathe. Thank you, I said to Him. That's a sign even I can understand.

The doctors made me drink things and rubbed stuff into my skin, all of which made the pain worse but did nothing about the swelling. After a bit I thanked them and told them to go away. The last thing I wanted was for them to cure me, at least not until Stilian was back home with his army intact.

And the news was good. Stilian had encountered a Robur raiding party, five thousand strong, heading for Beal Defour. He surrounded them with horse-archers and drove them like sheep onto the spearpoints of the 5th lancers. Only a handful of the enemy survived, and his own losses were trivial.

The swelling moved into my neck, and then my head, making my eyes blurry. I sent for the doctors. That's perfectly normal, they said. Nothing to worry about, then, I said. Not quite, they told me. It's perfectly normal for your vision to blur when you're as seriously ill as you are. Look on the bright side, though; your heart will probably give way before you go blind.

Thank you, I said, and I thought about poor Nico. The Divine Clemency of the Emperor, only in reverse. But divine clemency was what I'd prayed for, and if my prayers were granted I could ask for no more.

THEY WOKE ME up to tell me the news. Stilian and his entire army were dead.

I tried to get up, but there weren't enough people to help me. I fell on the floor, which was agony. They fetched a doctor, who said I wasn't to move for at least an hour on any account. So I received the messenger flat on my back, and hardly able to think straight for the pain.

The messenger was one Aelian Boutzes, a colonel in the lancers. He'd been sent off to reconnoitre, but he got lost, and by the time he found his way back it was all over. He had no idea what had happened, but there was our camp, swarming with Robur, and dead men everywhere, very few of them Robur. He pulled out quick sharp and galloped off to find the survivors. It was a flat plain. He didn't find any.

He spent the rest of the day avoiding Robur scouts, and the night trying to figure out what to do. Just before dawn he rode back, and saw the remains of the biggest harvest festival the Robur had celebrated for a very long time. Then he headed straight back to the City. It was just possible, he said, that a few hundred of Stilian's men had made it, but he doubted it very much. If there'd been any significant number of survivors, in that terrain he'd have seen them. And so, of course, would the Robur. No, he said, it was far more likely that he and his men were the only survivors. In which case, he added, there was nothing apart from a bit of geography between the Robur and the City.

It wasn't easy for me to talk right then. Drawing breath was like drawing water from a very deep well. But I asked him; so who's the most senior officer in the army right now?

He looked at me, very sad. That would probably be me, he said.

WELL, HE EXPLAINED later, strictly speaking that wasn't true. But he was from the six families himself (younger son, junior branch, but he obviously knew what he was talking about) and he could pretty well guarantee that as soon as the news of the disaster reached the remaining field armies—the ones Stilian hadn't marched off to their deaths—their commanders would immediately withdraw to their home provinces with an view to defending them in depth, and let the City burn, if so be it. As far as the six families were concerned, the army was the empire and the empire was the army, and wherever there was an army in being, that was the capital city and all the provinces. The City was just some place where money went to and never came back from, and idiotic parasites dictated bloody stupid orders to an army of eunuchs, more often than not sending brave men to their deaths. Let it burn, in other words. Who gives a damn?

But there's a quarter of a million people here, I told him. He shrugged. Omelettes and eggs, he said. That's how my cousins will see it, anyhow, he added quickly. As of now, there's no army. And no officers.

Except you, I said.

He gave me a please-don't-do-this look. I'm only a colonel, he said. And besides, like I just told you—

There's the palace guard, I said. That's eight thousand men.

Last we heard, said Aelian, as gently as he could, there were a hundred sixty thousand Robur. And Stilian was right. The only way you can beat them is overwhelming force.

I nodded. So if I asked you to lead the palace guard against them, you'd refuse.

I can't refuse, he said, not a direct order. But do you know what the Robur do to their prisoners?

Eat them, I said, yes, I know.

He shook his head. Not the high-ranking ones, he said, not the kings and princes and generals. What they do is, they get a round wooden post, about eight feet long, two or two and a half inches diameter, and they put a nice sharp point on it. They ram the pointy end about eighteen inches up your arse, then they plant the other end two feet in the ground. It's reckoned to be the most painful way a man can die, and it usually takes about six to eight hours. And it's no good your friends rescuing you, because by then the damage is done, all that happens is you live another twelve hours or so in unimaginable pain. I'll go if you tell me to, he went on, but on balance I'd rather not.

Later, I asked Bemba if it was true. He nodded. But they only do that to their worse enemies, he said; sorcerors and traitors and anyone who brings dishonour on the king. Like we have? I asked. Yes, he said

THAT WAS ALL I could manage that day. While I was trying to get some sleep, Edax came to see me.

I hadn't set eyes on him since they made me emperor. In fact, I seemed to remember giving explicit orders. Keep him the hell away from me, I think I might have said. But there he was, looking pale and thin but otherwise more or less normal. You're ill, he said.

So they tell me, I said.

He nodded and sat down on my bed. Are you going to die?

I don't know, I told him. The doctors say, sooner or later all this bulk will collapse my heart. Or I may suddenly get better.

He frowned. You look terrible, he said. Look, if you die, does that mean I'm emperor?

No, I said.

I think it does, he said. You don't have any kids, and I'm your only relative. Well, there's Nico, but he's blind and he's got no cock, and the law says that means you can't be emperor. I've got a cock, he said. I'm qualified.

Have him poisoned, they'd told me, or put away somewhere, a nice quiet island or a monastery on a mountaintop, the ones where they raise and lower visitors in a basket. I was shocked. He's my brother, I told them.

I'm emperor, I told him, because I married the old emperor's daughter.

Fine, he said, I'll do that. But I don't think it's necessary, strictly speaking. I think, soon as you die, it just sort of happens. Look, why don't you get that clerk of yours to look it up? Never hurts to be prepared. You know, in case the worst happens.

Listen to me, I said. I'm sorry. About what happened with Nico. I had no choice.

He shrugged. Water under the bridge, he said. You're the boss now, that's what matters. But if anything were to happen to you, I think I ought to know where I stand. Continuity, he said. It's essential for the well-being of the empire.

To everything there is a purpose, Scripture says, and everything is useful under the Sun. Except for my brother Edax. I'll ask Bemba to look into it, I said. And I did.

No, he told me, there's not a great deal you can do, unless you want him killed or blinded. Actually, he's quite right. He would be the lawful heir.

Me on the Imperial throne, with Edax by my side. This is why. I never knew He had a sense of humour.

I SENT FOR colonel Aelian. I want you to take command of the City guard, I told him, while I'm away.

He looked at me. You're going somewhere, he said.

Bemba will be City Prefect, I said, but most likely everyone will give him a hard time, because of who he is, so I want you to look after him. You'll do that for me, won't you?

He didn't like the idea of nursemaiding a Robur eunuch, but he'd already refused one direct order. Of course, he said. Where are you going?

Thank you, I said. You've set my mind at rest.

Stilian had been the colonel-in-chief of the Guards, and he didn't have a second-in-command. Or rather he had eight, each leading a battalion of a thousand men. I sent for them. We're going north, I told them.

There was an awkward silence. Excuse me, your majesty, one of them said eventually, but the Guards never leave the City.

Talking hurt me and tired me out. The duty of the Guards, I said, is to guard the person of the Emperor. Yes? They nodded. And the emperor is going north, I told them. So you're coming too.

Another long silence. May I ask where we're going?

To fight the Robur, I said.

They looked at each other. They weren't born-and-bred sons of the six families. They were working soldiers who'd spent their life in the army and gradually worked their way up, from junior subalterns to majors. Bloody stupid orders that got you killed were their natural predator, like foxes are with rabbits. Didn't mean they had to like it. Do I understand, one of them said, that your majesty will be leading the army in person?

I was getting tired of the conversation. Unless one of you wants to do it.

No volunteers. Does your majesty have any military experience?

I sighed. No, I said. But while I've been lying here, my clerk has read me a couple of good books about strategy, and if I don't shame you into going, you won't go. Or if you do, you'll find an excuse to stop somewhere and wait till the Robur have sacked the City and gone back home. Which is fair enough, you've got a duty to your men. But your duty to me comes first. Doesn't it?

I could see what was going through their heads. There's nobody here but us, we could hold a pillow over his face and then tell everyone his heart gave out. Nico would have done it like a shot. Doesn't it, I repeated. They nodded. But with respect, your majesty, one of them said, you must be out of your mind.

THEY FILLED A cart with goose feathers. It was bearable, most of the time.

Even so, I didn't enjoy the journey north. The Great Military Road, which the old emperor's great-grandfather built to be the main artery of the empire, hadn't had any money spent on it for about forty years, there being no money to spend, and the farmers had taken to robbing the paving-slabs to build walls and barns. I must do something about it, I thought, and then it occurred to me that, one way or another, I wouldn't be around long enough. That bothered me. You spend your life thinking, it's all right, I'll do something about this or that later, when I've got five minutes, I'll put it all right. Then suddenly you're like a man setting out on a long journey, and just as the ship casts off, he remembers all the things he forgot to pack.

I'd left Bemba behind to mind the store, but he'd found me a countryman and colleague of his, the only other Robur in the Service. His name was Sidoco (actually his name was Buffalo With A Split Horn, but life's too short) and he was a year or so older than me, a big, strong man. Bemba had made him swear by his honour to defend me to the death, which made me feel uncomfortable. Look, I said, if it comes to anything like that, run like hell. But he shook his head and explained that if he did that, his spirit would be cursed and he'd probably be reborn as a cockroach, and he despised cockroaches.

The Robur, Sidoco told me, live in huge wagons, with wheels taller than a man. These wagons are the only homes they have, or want; so when they go to war, their wives and children and sheep and goats and cows all go with them, and when the men are fighting, they form the wagons in a circle with the livestock in the middle. The wagons are so massively built, they're as good as a city wall, and a few good archers can defend them against an army. They despise settled people, he said, and the only reason they hadn't invaded the Empire long ago was that we didn't have anything they wanted. Wealth to them means women, children and livestock; they're polygamous, and treat anyone's children as their own, because they need the manpower. So, when a man kills his enemy, he takes his family as his own, and everybody seems quite happy about the arrangement. They don't eat meat, apart from their dead enemies; they reckon rearing living things for slaughter is barbaric. Who'd take something as graceful as an antelope or a partridge, they say, and turn it into shit? One of the reasons they fight so well is, they aren't really afraid of death. They believe in reincarnation, and the purpose of life is to live and die well, to earn merit, to be born into a better status next time round. So they don't understand about ambition. Your position in society isn't something you earn for yourself—at least you do, but not in this lifetime—and trying to improve on what you've been allotted is the most appalling blasphemy, and all it'll get you is a short, horrible life as a beetle next turn of the wheel. I have to admit, I liked the sound of the Robur. A lot of what they thought and how they went about things made a certain degree of sense, and it irked me that I was duty bound to wipe them off the face of the earth. Still, not much chance of that.

The eight battalion commanders asked me what my plan of campaign was. I told them I didn't have one, but I was open to suggestions.

At least it was over relatively quickly. At this point, the Robur had split into two roughly equal parties, about eighty thousand fighting men in each. One party had gone east, to sack Macestre. The other struck south, with a view to clearing up the string of big towns along the north bank of the Redwater before rejoining their friends for the main assault on the City. It was the southern party that found us, as we struggled through the mountain passes at Cans Juifrez.

The Robur realised that they had us exactly where they wanted us. If they waited for us to come down into the plain, there was a risk—small, but you never know—that our cavalry might work some miracle and carve them up. In the mountains, our cavalry were useless. A large part of tactical genius is taking advantage of the critical moment. An hour after the news of our arrival reached the wagons, eighty thousand Robur warriors were running—literally running—up the mountainside to catch us before we could slip away.

When they got there, they could see the way our minds had been working. We were waiting for them in a superb defensive position, a canyon with steep sides, only one narrow way in, and there we'd deployed the finest heavy infantry in the world, drawn up in phalanx. It was, they conceded, the best anyone could have done, in our position, given our pathetically small numbers. And yes, it'd be difficult, and their losses would be heavy, but they outnumbered us ten to one. And true, the Imperial heavy infantryman wears the best armour skill and money can provide, but the Robur archers are the best in the world, and their bows are very strong.

They shot at us. We knelt behind our shields, and the arrows mostly didn't penetrate. They charged. We drove them back. Shooting and kneeling, charging and repulsing; it was a long day, and come nightfall, very little to show for it. But during the evening, Robur scouts came in and said they'd found a narrow track that led round the back of the canyon. If the army split into two, and half of them went round the back way, when the Sun rose they'd be able to take us in front and rear, and that would be that.

So that's what they did; and the guards fought like heroes, to the very last man, and then it was all over. And then the Robur, carefully counting the dead, for obvious reasons, made a disturbing discovery. There were only a thousand dead guards. But the scouts had seen eight thousand men marching into the other end of the canyon.

DEAR GOD, IT shouldn't have worked. The battalion commanders told me it wouldn't, that I was a fool and I'd get them all killed. I said, yes, it's a stupid idea, so please, give me a better one. And they couldn't, so we did it my way, and it worked.

One thousand men—volunteers, God forgive me—stayed to defend the pass, while the other seven thousand slipped out down the funny little goat track, crept past the Robur and dashed like lunatics to get to the wagons before the Robur figured they'd been had. We made it, and in good time, even though we were hindered by having to lug me along on a stretcher. Eliminating the sentries on the wagons was an awkward moment, a point at which the whole thing could have gone horribly wrong, but the guards are good at that sort of thing, and we managed it. In half an hour, in the dark, we got control of the wagons, and when the Sun rose, we had all the women and kids rounded up and roped together. And now, one of the battalion commanders said to me, we can negotiate.

I shook my head. No, I said.

But that's crazy, he said. We've got them by the balls. The Robur love their kids. We can get out of this alive, if we play our cards right.

No, I told him. All right, let's suppose we strike a deal and they honour it, which they won't, because it's no sin to break a promise to the likes of us. Let's suppose we do a deal, and they go away. And next year, they come back. Sorry, I told him, but we've got to do it properly. He closed his eyes and counted to ten, and stalked away to organise the defence.

We let the scouts get up nice and close, so they could see we had the women and children up close to the wagons. That way, if the best archers in the world shot at us with their wonderful cane bows, they'd be shooting their own families. So instead they charged us with their spears and scimitars, and we shot them with our second-best archers and second-best bows as they came. They charged six times, and then they faltered, because suddenly there were so very few of them left; and then I gave the order to mount up, and our cavalry burst out of there and slaughtered them, until they were all dead.

I say we. All I did was lie there, in my feathers, listening to the horrors and not knowing what was going on. Then something happened—later they told me a Robur managed to scramble onto a wagon, he got shot and fell on me. Anyway, it hurt like hell and I passed out, and when I came round I couldn't see.

The Divine Clemency of the Emperor, I believe they call it.

WE SPARED ONE man, just one; and we sent him to tell the other Robur army to come and collect their widows and orphans, and not to come bothering us again.

(And that was the good part; because wealth to the Robur is women and children and livestock, and suddenly the survivors were twice as rich as they had been; so they went home perfectly satisfied, and with honour. I imagine they'll be back in thirty years or so, once a new generation has grown up, but that's a problem for another day. The war is never over.)

The doctors told me my sight would return, could well return, might possibly return, until I told them to leave me alone. The bump I got in the battle did me no good at all, and then it rained and I got soaked to the skin, which more or less finished me. The ride back to the City was no fun at all. They tell me my heart stopped once, and Sidoco jumped on me and punched me and got it going again; and I had a stroke, and various other unpleasant things. None of which I minded, but I couldn't make anyone else see that. Not that it mattered, at that.

What I wanted was for them to put me on a ship to the island where I'd sent Nico, so he could tell me what he thought of me before I died, but the doctors wouldn't allow it; and besides, I can't imagine I'd have lasted as far as the island, and politically it was important that I die in the City. Talking of which; Edax will almost certainly be emperor. The soldiers kept telling me to have him killed while there was still time, all the way from the Redwater to the City, and I knew they were giving me good advice, but I couldn't make myself do it, he's my brother; this is why. When I die, in the City, he'll be there to take the crown off the bed and stick it on his head, and then he'll be safe for a little while, until people get sick to death of him, which probably won't be very long. I hope not, anyway; the less time he's in charge, the less harm he'll be able to do. What happens after he's gone, I simply can't imagine. Those are other prayers, for someone else to make. I can't do everything myself; and what little I've done, I've done badly.

But—that's why I've told Bemba to write on the top of his scroll, *My Beautiful Life*. All my life I've done terrible, bad things. I've stolen, I've murdered, I've betrayed. I had my wife locked up in a tower, and I blinded my brother. Sometimes I ask why; and the answer stays the same. Where was I when He laid the foundations of the earth? This is why. I know I've been given the answer, and I know I've never managed to understand it. But that's my fault. And then I was given the sign, a sign so clear, even a fool like me could see it. And it was the last thing I ever saw, which pleases me. Anything else after that would've been a dreadful anticlimax.

Beauty is in the eye of the beholder; if thine eye offends thee, pluck it out. It's been a beautiful life, one way and another.